# When Loving You Isn't Enough

## An Urban Romance

**A Novel by**
**Nikalos**

Text **MAJOR** to **22828** to join our maili

list!

To submit a manuscript for our review, email us at

submissions@majorkeypublishing.com

***Published by Major Key Publishing LLC***

*www.majorkeypublishing.com*



**Contains explicit language & adult themes suitable for ages 16+**

Be sure to LIKE our Major Key Publishing

page on Facebook!

## Dedication

To the woman who has stolen my heart, I love you.

# Chapter 1

## Monica

I stepped out of the car and paused for a brief second as I stared at my mini-mansion. I hit the alarm on my BMW 750Li and glanced around. I could tell that my neighbors were tucked in for the night. I lived in one of the most upscale neighborhoods in Albany, Georgia. You could leave your doors unlocked and not have to worry about anyone breaking into your place. I really loved my neighborhood. As I turned the knob on my front door, my feet didn't even get over the threshold before I was quickly snatched up, which took me by surprise. I dropped the shopping bags I had in my hand, and my heart started beating rapidly.

"Where the fuck you been!" Jihad yelled angrily in my face while pushing me into the couch.

"I was with Zykiah. She wanted me to go shopping with her."

As I was talking, I could feel his hot breath breathing down my neck. My neck hairs were standing up at attention. Jihad was six feet two, dark-skinned, and muscular. I was only five feet tall with a small frame. The only thing big on me was my round ass.

"Why didn't you call me and let me know where the fuck you were?" Jihad asked while pointing his finger in my face and poking my forehead.

"Because I knew you'd been working all day long, and I didn't want to bother you," I said while trying to fix my clothes.

Jihad started pacing back and forth throughout the living room. I was scared to death, standing there with thousands of thoughts in my head. I was lost, but I knew I had to defuse the situation before things got out of hand. My palms were sweating like crazy.

"Baby, calm down. You don't want to get yourself all worked up," I pleaded while putting my arms around him.

"Get the fuck off me!" Jihad yelled, pushing me away from him.

"Why are you acting like this?" I cried out.

"What!" Jihad yelled and gave me a menacing look.

My heart dropped to my stomach. In the back of my mind, I knew some bullshit was about to jump off.

"Baby," I approached him very cautiously.

"Baby, I went shopping with Zykiah for a homecoming gift for Aubrey," I explained. Jihad heard every single word I said but just stood there and stared at me for a good thirty seconds. The way he looked at me seemed like he wanted me dead. He put his index finger on his chin as he stared daggers at me.

"So, you think I'm fucking crazy?" he sarcastically asked with a devilish grin on his face. I was about to speak, but he put his hands up and signaled for me not to. I did as I was told. I could see the veins in his forehead.

"So, you went shopping with Zykiah, right?" He interrogated me while pointing his finger for an answer.

"Yes," I answered quickly.

"Okay," he said and smiled.

I knew right then that he had some bullshit on his mind.

"So, Zykiah wanted you the help her pick out a gift for some dude named Aubrey, huh?" I nodded my head in agreement. He just made a gesture with his two fingers like "whatever." I felt like a suspect in a murder trial.

*I understood how O.J. Simpson felt when he was on that murder trial,* I thought to myself.

"You think I'm crazy, huh? Your red ass been out fucking some nigga," Jihad accused me furiously.

He grabbed a wine glass off the dining room table and threw it against the wall. The glass shattered everywhere. I put my hand up to prevent the glass from getting into my eyes. Jihad's whole demeanor had changed in a split second. He started cursing at me like a hoe out in the streets. His words cut through me like razor blades. Jihad approached me, and it felt like my body went numb instantly. I could feel my heart racing through my entire body.

"Honey, I was with Zyk—"

*WHACK!* Jihad landed a blow directly on my face. His powerful blow made my fragile body hit the floor instantly. I was even more scared.

"Bitch, you think I'm fucking stupid?"

"No!" I cried out while holding my face and backing up close to the wall.

*WHAM!* Jihad hit me again. This time he showed no mercy. His swing connected with my eye in the matter of a second. I blacked out for a quick second. Jihad threw one blow after another, sending pain all over my face.

"So, you went shopping for another nigga with my fucking money?" Jihad punched me with an extremely hard jab to the center of my face.

I couldn't do anything but curl up in the corner and feel the pain he was inflicting on me. Jihad was in an extreme rage. I laid in the corner like a rag doll. I thought it wouldn't stop. Every time he spoke, pain followed. He released all of his rage on me and left me there like I was nothing.

"Why, God, am I going through this?" I asked as I lay there and observed Jihad straightening himself up.

I watched him grab a bottle of Jack Daniels off the minibar and head for the door. He jumped in his Camaro Z128 and got ghost.

I lay on the floor until I had the strength to get up. Tears fell nonstop from my eyes. My face felt like horses had been prancing on it. I couldn't understand why he treated me like this.

"God, help me. Please!" I cried out loud.

Finally, when I got up, I went to look in the mirror to see how badly bruised my face was. I looked in amazement at the bruises my ungrateful husband had put on me. I suffered a swollen face and two black eyes that could be seen a mile away due to my light complexion.

I was a very high-yellow woman. In grade school, people would tease me saying that my daddy had to be the milkman. In the dirty south, that meant your daddy was white. I had parents that were God-fearing people. They taught me that when things got hard, go pray to God. I didn't have many friends due to me being very smart and having nice clothes. I met Jihad in the tenth grade. That's when things started the change for me. Jihad was so sweet and charming. A lot of people couldn't understand how we were so attracted to each other since we were total opposites. Jihad was the only man I had ever slept with. I believed in keeping a good reputation. Plus, I had the man of my dreams.

As I was looking in the mirror, I kept repeating, "Why, Lord?"

I was a spiritual person even though Jihad was the total opposite. I still asked God to change his mind as well as his heart. I got down on my knees to talk to the man above. Before I could get a word out, my phone went off. The first time, I ignored the call. I was not in the mood to talk to anyone until the caller called back.

"Hello?" I answered, sounding frustrated.

"Ewwww, that's how you answer the phone?" Zykiah asked.

"Naw, I just got a lot on my mind."

"Like what, Mo?"

"I don't want to put my burdens on you."

"Really, bitch? Mo, don't play with me," she demanded.

"Bu—"

Zykiah interrupted me. "But nothing. We been girls

since they canceled *Martin*, so don't play with me."

Zykiah and I had been best friends since we were in diapers. We used to call each other sisters in school. Zykiah's mother used to watch me while my parents were at work. When my parents died in a bad car accident, I went to live with my granny for a little while until she passed away. Just when I thought I was going to a group home, Zykiah's mother took me in and raised me like I was one of her own. It was a big change for me, but I liked the love they showed me. It felt like home to me. It was never a boring moment growing up with Zykiah.

"Well, me and Jihad got into it again," I confessed.

A pound of tears dropped from my eyes onto the phone.

"What!" Zykiah screamed into the phone. "Did that fuck nigga put his fucking hands on you?"

"We had a little fight."

I felt so empty inside, and I didn't know what to do. My world wasn't supposed to be like this.

"That fuck nigga!" she shouted.

*WHAM!* I heard a loud thump in her background. "I just want to put some hot lead in that bitch ass nigga," Zykiah said as I heard her let out a large breath of air into the receiver.

“I don’t know what to do,” I cried into the phone.

I sniffled and wiped the tears away as I waited to hear what Zykiah had to say.

“Shit! Put a couple of bullets into that pussy ass nigga’s dome,” Zykiah suggested.

“No... no,” I pleaded, gripping the bible I was holding even tighter.

“And why not?” she asked.

“Because that wouldn’t be right. We got to pray for better days,” I preached.

Jihad and Zykiah never got along. She tried to protect me from him, but Jihad somehow had his game down pat when it came to me. His charm was too strong. I couldn’t resist him.

“You tell me about God all the time. How much do you have to suffer until God changes his heart?”

“I know you don’t like how I look at life. We just gotta keep God in our life, and I know we will see better days.”

Zykiah wasn’t a religious person. She felt she controlled her destiny. She always asked me if there was a God, why would he allow things to happen to kids and old people? Her theory was that there was no such thing as God, and we, as humans, were over our own destiny.

Zykiah was a straight up project ass chick that didn't mind peeling a nigga's cap back. After we talked for over an hour, we both disconnected the call. Instead of crying more tears, I ran some hot water in the tub so I could relax and forget about today.

# Chapter 2

## Zykiah

I was sitting on my queen size bed thinking about my friend.

"Damn, Mo, I hate you going through this with that lame ass nigga," I said to myself.

So many things ran through my mind, making me reminisce about my last husband, Dewayne.

One cold Saturday night around midnight, Dewayne came through the door smelling like a tub of beer. He was so intoxicated that he didn't even see me standing in the corner of the living room.

"Wayne!" I yelled, causing him to lose all the balance he had left in his legs. *WHAM!* Wayne fell face first on the coffee table. I rushed to his rescue.

"Wayne! Wayne!" I cried out because he'd hit the floor kind of hard.

"Mmmmm..." he moaned out with blood leaking from his face.

I grabbed a towel to clean him up. I used all my strength to put him on the couch. Dewayne was six feet tall. He was the size of a polar bear and as black as night.

"Baby, are you ok?" I tried to finish cleaning him up.

"Wayne!"

"Sherry, leave me alone." He pushed me away.

WHACK! I slapped the taste out of his mouth.

"Sherry! What the fu—" I threw an Ali uppercut to his face.

Dewayne snapped out of his drunkenness.

"Woman!" he said as he grabbed my shoulder.

I was furious, and I quickly broke loose.

"So, you still fucking your baby mama?" I demanded an answer from him as I pounded my fists into his chest and tears fell down my face. I wanted to punch the fuck out of him again. I was so hot. "I knew you were still fucking that bitch."

Dewayne didn't respond. He just stood there looking dumb. He walked toward me, but I stopped him in his tracks, letting him know it was the sofa tonight. I went to the bedroom and slammed the door. I didn't sleep much. I just stared at the ceiling the whole night. I couldn't shed another tear. When I got up to pee, I heard Wayne in there snoring like a huge grizzly bear. I stood over him, staring at this low-life ass. The longer I watched him rest, the more I hated the ground he walked on. Images popped into my head of him and that bitch kissing then him coming home and kissing me.

Before I knew it, I had a six-inch butcher knife in my hand. I stabbed that dirty motherfucker thirty times without even blinking twice. Blood was all over me. I had lost it. My whole body was shaking. I called my cousin afterward, so he could come and get rid of his body. I had no remorse for what I had done. To this day, I didn't care that I had killed Wayne. In my eyes, he deserved to die because he had broken my heart.

The ringing of my phone snapped me back to reality.

"Hello?" I answered, using my white woman voice.

"Hey, beautiful."

"Hey, Boo Bear," I said with excitement in my voice.

"How's my baby doing today?" Aubrey asked.

"I'm great, baby, now that I'm talking with you."

I couldn't control myself. Every time I heard Aubrey's deep seductive voice, it made my pussy moist.

"That's good. I got some great news for you."

"What, baby?" I asked anxiously, waiting for what he was about to tell me.

"Calm down. I'm just about to tell you. I'm gonna pull up on you this weekend."

"Yaaayyy!" I screamed into the phone, jumping up and down.

"Are you going to show me a good time?

"Of course. You know I got you, baby."

"When I get in town, I will hit you up."

"Aye, Aubrey, c'mon," a co-worker in the background said to him.

"I gotta get back to work. Talk to you later. Don't forget to text me your address."

"You know I'm on that already," I responded with a big smile on my face.

"You better stay out of trouble."

"I been bad. You need to come punish this pussy," I flirted.

"Trust me, I will, baby. I love you. Gotta go," he said before he hung up the phone.

I was satisfied that my man would finally be coming back home. We had been talking for about six months. Due to his career as a truck driver, I didn't see him often. After getting off the phone with Aubrey, my body began to ache for his touch. I grabbed my vibrator, laid down on the bed, and began to please myself until I went to La La Land.

# Chapter 3

## Monica

Pulling up at Carter's Grill, the place was slightly packed. Jihad was taking me out for lunch. We hadn't done this in a long time, so I didn't complain. I glanced at Jihad and noticed that he was ending his phone call.

"You ready?" I asked him while touching his hand.

He shut the engine off as we proceeded to the entrance. The line was not that long, and I was glad of that. Our waiter was medium brown in complexion, tall, slim, and looked to be about six feet in height.

"Thanks for taking me out for lunch," I stated.

"No problem," he replied.

When the waiter came with our menus, I placed my order first. I got the Southern smoked ribs with baked beans, potato salad, a glass of iced tea, and a side of peach cobbler. Jihad got the crispy fried chicken with yellow rice, collard greens, cornbread, and a cup of lemonade. I caressed his hand, trying to make eye contact with him. Somehow, his mind was elsewhere.

"Jay, I want our marriage to get back to how it used to be," I said, gripping his hand tighter.

He just stared at me like I was speaking some type of foreign language or something.

"Why don't we walk around the park like we used to and just spend some time with one another?"

"Monica, don't start all that," he shot back, pulling his hand away.

Before I could say anything, the waiter brought our food to the table. The ribs were glazed perfectly with barbecue sauce. I wanted to just dig in, but I didn't want to stain my white sundress. Jihad's chicken smelled great.

"Thanks, sir," I said to the waiter as he walked away.

"You're welcome, ma'am," he replied with a huge smile.

"Your food looks delicious," I told Jay, but he quickly ignored my comment.

"I will be back," he said as he walked toward the restroom.

I sat there as I waited for him to come back so we could say grace. My phone started to vibrate. It was Zykiah sending me a text.

**Zykiah:** *I Hope everything is good with you :-)*

I texted her back and told her I was having fun with Jay. I was just about to exit out of my messages when I noticed Jihad had gotten back from the bathroom, and he had a stoned expression on his face.

"Let's say grace, honey," I suggested.

Jihad took a seat before he shook his head at me.

"You know I'm not into all of that bullshit," he said with a stank attitude while driving his fork into his food. Instead of fussing with him, I said a small prayer to myself.

The rest of our lunch was silent until the polite waiter came with the bill. Jihad paid the bill, and I made sure to leave the waiter a tip along with a Bible booklet. Jihad gave me a hateful look when he noticed that I had left the waiter a Bible booklet.

Once we got in the car, he started it up. I could see the irritation on his face. I couldn't understand why he was so angry with me. *I didn't do anything wrong,* I thought to myself. The whole trip home, the only thing I heard was the wind coming from the cracked window.

Finally, we arrived at the house, and he turned off the car. He hopped out and stormed into the house, leaving me behind in the dark car.

"God, help me," I whispered into the darkness.

I gathered my belongings and was just about to step out of the car when my car door opened. I was shocked to see Jihad standing there looking at me with his fists balled up.

*WHAM!* My body hit the ground.

"You think I'm stupid, bitch?" Jihad asked very aggressively.

I had dirt and grass all in my hair. He slapped me across the face. The pain ran through my body. I was helpless. I tried to fight back, but he was too strong for me. Another slap came followed by another one.

"You still ain't learned yet, huh?" He grabbed a handful of my hair and dragged me into the house.

As he gripped my hair, I tried hitting his hand, but he didn't let my hair go. He only gripped it tighter.

"Oh, you wanna fight back, huh?" he asked while punching me in my face. My face was numb. I could taste blood coming out of my mouth. Once we made it inside of the house, he grabbed my phone out of my purse and smashed it against the wall into a million pieces.

"Stop, Jihad!" I put my hand up for mercy.

"Why can't you just be a good bitch?" he said, charging at me.

The only thing I knew to do was run. I ran to the back room and closed the door as fast as I could, but he was too quick. He pushed the door and threw me down. I had no earthly idea what he was about to do. Jihad grabbed my hair and pounded my face with his fist. The more I tried to struggle, the crueler the punishment.

"Jih—" He cut me off with another blow to the face.

"Shut the fuck up!" he yelled.

He ripped off my dress and then my panties.

"No, Jihad, stop!" I pleaded.

He was in such a rage that sweat was dripping from his face.

"When you act like a slut, I'm gonna treat you like a nasty slut," he said, pulling out his dick.

He flipped me over and entered my ass.

"Ahhhh!" I screamed out.

It was painful. Every stroke was harder than the first one. I never had anything in my ass before, and I was in total shock.

"That's how you want it, right!" he yelled, pushing deep inside of me.

He pulled my hair, making my ear reach his mouth.

"You're nothing but a stupid ass bitch!"

He pushed me to the floor then jacked his dick in my face. I felt like dying right then and there. After he was done, he jumped in the shower. I found the strength to lift myself up from the floor. I was sore all over, and my asshole was burning. There was blood running from it. I stared at myself in the mirror.

“My life isn’t supposed to be like this,” I told myself.

I grabbed my keys and hit the auto start to crank my car up so that it would be running when I got out the door. I headed for the front door, jumped in my car, and took off. I had no clue where I was going. I don’t know how long I drove before I finally arrived at my destination.

# Chapter 4

## Zykiah

*BOOM! BOOM!*

"What the fuck!" I yelled, rolling out of bed and trying to figure out who the hell was at my door at three o'clock in the motherfucking morning. When I opened the door, my heart fell to the floor. Monica was standing there with tears and blood coming out of her mouth.

"What the fuck happened?"

I was heated. I wanted to kill that motherfucker. I wrapped my arms around her to give her some comfort because she was shaking really bad.

"Go take them clothes off and freshen up," I said to her.

Monica hopped in the shower as I headed toward my bedroom to pull out my .45. I had a lot of frustration built up in me at this point. I was ready to unleash my wrath on that fuck nigga. The only reason I hadn't was due to my bitch being so in love with him. I was in my closet digging for my bullets when Monica stepped out of the bathroom wrapped in a towel.

"What are you doing with that gun?" she asked

curiously.

“I got some bullets in here for J-I-H-A-D!” I broke it down to her.

“No! That can’t be possible,” she protested.

“I can’t sit here and let this pussy nigga think it’s okay to hit you, Mo!” I stated.

“I know things are crazy, but I gotta deal with this situation another way,” she protested.

*I guess I'm going to let her do her, but if that nigga comes wrong, I'm not gonna hesitate to blast that fool,* I thought to myself.

Monica decided to sleep in the guest bedroom for the night, and it wasn’t long before I heard her snoring. I just stared at the ceiling the rest of the morning because I couldn’t fall back to sleep. When I did doze off, I woke up to repeated knocks at my door. I knew someone had to have lost their fucking mind. Once I saw who it was, it sparked a flame in me that was starting to burn out of me.

“What the fuck you want?” I asked Jihad with the barrel pointed in his face. I stared him in his eyes. I could sense the bitch in him. I had a tight grip on the gun.

“Where she at!” Jihad yelled, trying to look around me.

“Why?” I shot back.

- I HATE MY JOB
But I love the
vision. (love the vision
But HATE MY JOB)

- Your trauma is apart
of your survivor

your plan is your
vision on paper

Appendix: C

## Distribution List

Date:_01.09.22_

**5S EXT: 7258**

**4S EXT: 7152**

Time: C SHIFT Facility: BCBIC

| umber | Location | Show Y/N Circle One | Comments--- use codes | Patient's Signature Verifying Medication Given |
|---|---|---|---|---|
| 868606 | 5S,A,17,A | Y / N | | |
| 2640334 | 5S,A,17,B | Y / N | | |
| 1430851 | 5S,A,2,B | Y / N | | |
| 3418642 | 5S,A,20,C | Y / N | | |
| 1312168 | 5S,A,23,C | Y / N | | |
| 2682670 | 5S,A,4,A | Y / N | | |
| 998079 | 5S,A,5,B | Y / N | | |
| 1201000 | 5S,A,8,B | Y / N | | |

“Stop with the games,” he said while calling Mo’s name throughout the house.

“Only game I’m ‘bout to play is seeing how long it’s going to take your bitch ass to stop breathing.”

I just wanted him to try something. I didn’t hesitate to take my gun off safety. This time, his punk ass put his hands up in surrender. I had a grin on my face. I’d been waiting for this moment for a long time. I think my pussy even got wet. Right before I was about to pull the trigger, I heard my bitch’s voice.

“Kiah, no!” She rushed to me, grabbing the gun. “Don’t do it.”

Tears were streaming down her face. I was pissed off. I wanted to leave his ass leaking. I lowered the gun from his temple, but I still had it aimed at him.

“Baby, I’m sorry. Baby, come back home,” he said, whining like the little bitch that he was.

*I hope she leaves his ass standing there,* I thought to myself as I watched how the shit was playing out.

“Just come back. You know I can’t function without you.”

My girl didn’t respond. She just looked at him. My heart was doing flips.

“Yesss.” That’s all I was saying in my head.

"See you later," I spat as I broke up the little act he was putting on.

"I'm not going anywhere without my wife," he said, reaching out for her hand.

"Shit, was she your wife when you put your hands on her!" I yelled.

"Man, let me and my wife handle our marriage. Do me a favor, and stay out my damn business."

"Hold the fuck up, nigga. You don't demand shit up in this bitch."

"Hold up," Monica pleaded, putting her hands between us. "She's right. Don't come over here demanding nothing," Monica commented.

I was shocked to see my bitch talking like this.

"Kiah, let me see what he's talking about."

I just stood back and let her do her thing. I didn't want to, but the respect I had for her allowed me to listen to her.

"C'mon, baby," he said, reaching out for her hand.

"Look, Jihad, I'm tired of doing this with you," he tried to speak, but she cut him off.

I was like, "Go, girl!" in my Martin Payne voice.

"I'm coming home, but…"

He was cheesing and glancing at me. I just showed

him my fire and gave him a look that told him not fuck with me.

"I'm not coming back today. I need to think things over."

His face dropped to the ground. As Monica started walking him to the door, he said, "Mo, baby." He grabbed her arm, begging.

She paused for a second. I had never seen that side of her before, but I was soaking it all in. I loved every moment of it.

"When you coming home?" he asked.

"When the old Jihad comes back," she replied as she closed the door in his face.

I gave her a huge hug.

"I'm tired, Kiah," she said.

"I know you are, girl. I was about to blast his ass too."

"For real!"

"Hell yeah," I added.

We sat on the couch and turned to Lifetime and just watched movies all day. I told her she could stay as long as she wanted to. No matter what happened, I was always going to be in Monica's corner. Just before my mother passed away, I promised her that I was going to look after Monica and that was what I was going to do. There was no way in hell I was about to let anybody fuck with Monica because like I said earlier, Monica was my family.

# Chapter 5

## Monica

It was nearly 1:30 p.m. when I pulled into the parking space in front of Zykiah's condo and parked next to her Infiniti Q60 Coupe. I turned off my Aston Martin Rapides, slid out the car, and hit the alarm because I didn't trust these niggas around here. Jihad and I had been talking on the phone for the past week, but I still refused to see him. Every time he came around, Kiah ran him off with her gun. A bitch would be lying if I said I didn't miss Jihad. He was my husband, and I loved him with all my heart.

As I strolled to Kiah's front door, I noticed a small note on her car windshield.

"What in the hell is this?" I said to myself as I grabbed the note and read it.

*STAY THE FUCK AWAY FROM MY MAN, LAST WARNING!"* I glanced around. I felt like someone was watching me. I tucked the note in my purse and went into the house.

"Kiah! Kiah!" I yelled throughout the house, looking for her. She was nowhere to be found. I grabbed the remote, flopped down on the sofa, and began to flip through the channels. Kiah emerged from the back of the couch a few moments later and nearly scared my ass when she pulled my hair from the back.

"Sup, girl? Why you calling my name all crazy?" Kiah asked playfully.

"Bitch, you late," I shot back.

"What we got planned?" Kiah asked.

"Well, to be honest, I got a date tonight," I commented with a smile on my face.

"Bitch, it's about damn time you found somebody else," she said with excitement as she began to do her crazy dance.

"I'm going out with Jihad," I mumbled.

She paused.

"What? Hold up… repeat that. I need to know that I heard you correctly."

"Jihad wants to take me out. I miss him so much. This is the longest I have ever been away from him. You know how much I love him," I confessed.

"Girl! I told you that sorry piece of shit don't deserve you," Kiah preached.

"You just don't understand. I love him with all of my heart," I added.

"What I don't understand is how you allow him to treat you like this."

I didn't respond. I just sat there with a blank look on my face because her words impinged my heart.

"Mo, I'm going to be one thousand with you…"

Everything got silent. Her whole demeanor changed.

"You my bitch. I hate knowing that you get abused like this. You're a great woman, and you deserve the best."

I nodded my head as I looked away from my best friend. She walked over to where I was sitting and lifted my chin up so her eyes met mines.

"I just don't want you to get hurt. Shit, if I was into women, you know I would treat you like the queen that you are."

I swear Kiah knew all the right things to say to make me feel better. We embraced in a short hug. I stood up and was just about to head toward the kitchen to get me a drink of water when Kiah playfully smacked my ass.

We burst out laughing before we walked into the kitchen. She watched me grab a bottled water from the fridge.

"Real talk… you need to let him go," Kiah suggested.

"Kiah, he used to be a great man."

"Keyword *used*," she emphasized.

"I know."

"When that piece of shit started making all that money, that's when he started showing his ass. It ain't right what he doing to you, Mo. I don't know why you won't just let him go."

"Because I made a vow to God—until death do us part."

"God would have to understand this time because I don't want to wake up and see you on an episode of *Snapped*."

Kiah was my best friend, and I understood her concern for me. I just didn't understand what was going on with my life and how did Jihad and I got here. I knew deep in my heart that my faith in God would change things for the better. Kiah was just about to go in on my ass about why she felt I deserved better when I remembered the note that I stuck in my purse.

"Oh yeah, Kiah, I got something for you."

Kiah stopped her rant and began bouncing around showing all of her thirty-twos.

"Calm down. Don't get all happy-go-lucky because it's not like that."

I gave her the note. She read it and ripped it in half. She had a devilish smile on her face. I gave her a questioning look.

"Well, I guess I have pussy whipped a bitch's nigga. Apparently, she can't get no more dick from him," she said, bursting out laughing and twerking her ass.

I fell to the floor laughing my ass off.

"Kiah, you off the damn chain, girl!"

"Naw, I just keep it a hunnit!" We smacked hands on it.

"Well, while you're out with that busta, I'm gonna chill out."

She went to the back of the condo and closed her door softly. Kiah's words kept replaying in my head like a song on repeat, and I couldn't think of anything else. Instead of stressing, I got down on my knees and began to say a prayer.

"Lord, help my marriage. Change my husband's heart. Remove the darkness from his life. Give him the light to shine so bright. Amen."

When I stood up, Kiah was standing in the doorway and shaking her head at me.

"What you got going on?" she asked me, pulling me off the floor.

"Just asking God to give me what I need to help my marriage."

"I know what you need, Mo."

"What?"

"You need to shoot that motherfucker in the head," she suggested, posing like she was firing a shot.

I just looked at that crazy fool with my hands on my hips and my lips poked out.

"You know I can't do that. It won't be Godly."

"I guess, but I do know this…"

"What?" I asked, wondering what this fool had on her mind.

"God must be a pimp or something."

"Why you say that, fool?"

"Because you stay on your knees!" She burst out laughing.

I couldn't laugh at that fool. I gave her a look that said, "You're wrong for that."

"Let me stand over here because when he shoots lightning bolts your way, I'll be good." She opened her arms. "You know you a got a first-class ticket to hell."

She just smiled at me then put two fingers up for the devil horns.

*KNOCK! KNOCK!* I glanced at the clock.

“It must be Jihad,” I said with a nervousness in my voice.

When I opened the door, his cologne invaded my nostrils, and it drove me wild. I couldn’t lie, he was standing there looking sexy as hell. I could barely take my eyes off of him. I just wanted to jump into his arms and kiss his juicy lips.

Jihad was rocking a V-neck with a pair of dark denim jeans. He had a fresh cut that showed off his deep, silky waves with some bright diamond earrings in both ears.

“Hi, how are you, Monica?” He greeted me with a dozen roses.

He knew damn well I loved me some roses.

“I’m good, Jihad. Thanks for the flowers,” I responded as I motioned for Kiah to come grab the flowers.

They eyeballed each other for a split second, and my heart began to race. I prayed that these two didn’t get to fighting. I just wanted everyone to get along.

“Look, if she don’t come back the same way she leaves here, I promise you, I will fucking kill you,” she threatened as her eyes penetrated his. She kissed me on my cheek before walking away and didn’t even wait for Jihad to respond.

“You ready?” he asked with a smirk like he’d won the war.

I nodded my head.

When I stepped out the door, I noticed he had just gotten a new Rolls-Royce Dawn/Wraith. It was platinum-silver with white interior inside and the leather seats were trimmed in silver. I was very impressed when he opened the door for me. He had my favorite R&B song blasting through the speakers—Amerie’s “Nothing Like Loving You.”

Jihad and I talked and laughed about old times until we arrived at Emerald Coast, one of my favorite spots to eat, a few moments later. Emerald Coast was the first place Jihad had ever taken me when he and I first met. Jihad was acting like such a gentleman. I was beginning to think that God had finally come through and had taught him a lesson.

“Monica, thank you for letting me take you out,” he said and kissed me so passionately I felt like I was floating in midair.

Once we stepped into the restaurant, I was shocked when I learned that he had the place decorated just for me. I turned to him and gave him a small kiss on the cheek. He deserved that. I felt so special that words couldn't describe the emotions that were coursing throughout my body. I knew my baby would come back.

"Baby, I love you so much."

"I love you too."

When our lips met, I felt as if he and I could get through anything together.

"Excuse me, lovebirds." The hostess snapped us back into reality.

She led us to this booth with many roses covering it. I was speechless because I was loving all of it. All the prayers I sent to God had finally been answered. I tried to stop the tears, but I couldn't help it. I was in the happiest place ever. I took a picture of the moment. I even had the waiter take a picture of us together. We sat down, and she gave us our menus. I already knew what I wanted.

"I'm ready to order. I want the Shrimp Shack Platter," I told the waitress.

The waitress wrote my order down before staring at Jihad so she could take his order.

"I just want the Double Decker Chicken."

"Mo, I need you back at home with me."

Jihad stared into my eyes. I instantly became wet between my legs, and my clit was aching to be sucked.

My heart and body were screaming "yes," but my

mind was saying something different.

"I don't know yet," I said, looking him in his hazel eyes

"Why, babe? I miss you so much."

He caressed my hand. The craving I had for him was crazy.

"Don't get me wrong, I miss you like crazy, but you hurt me so bad," I responded.

"Babe, I know I been on some Grade A bullshit. I have changed. I need you."

He poked his lips out.

"Let's just see how the night ends, so be on your best behavior."

He smiled, and that's when the food came out. I was shocked when Jihad grabbed my hand and actually said grace. I knew he must have changed for real. I sat there thanking God the whole time. Once we finished eating our dinner, I had made up my mind. I knew what I wanted to do. When I told him I was coming back home, his whole face lit up. I was sure things were going to be okay.

We paid the bill and left the waitress a nice tip before we dipped out. Once we got in the house, he and I got straight down to business. I ripped his pants off and pulled down his boxers. I had been missing his dick like crazy.

After he was undressed, he kissed me on the mouth and bit my bottom lip gently. He then pulled my head down and commanded me to suck his dick. I started kissing the tip of his tool as I massaged his balls with my free hand. I made his dick disappear in my mouth, and he instantly began to moan.

"Mmm... yes..." He groaned as he held on to my head.

I sucked him until he filled my mouth with his creamy, thick nut. He picked me up and took me to the bedroom. We kissed the whole way there. Once my body hit the bed, he was on rock hard. When he slid between my legs and put his dick inside me, I lost all control and was ready for him to fuck me like he missed me.

"Shit, baby, just like that," I moaned while sucking on his neck.

He stroked even harder.

"Damn, this pussy good!" he yelled out, as he pumped me faster.

"This your pussy!" I yelled out to him.

"Damn right."

He slapped my thighs, and that gave me an extra

boost. I threw that pussy on him.

I flipped over, and I was ready to ride that monster. I straddled him, put my hands on his chest, and brought my ass up slow then back down. I did that about two times then I grinded down on it. His dick was up inside me, and it was filling me up.

"Ssss.... hmmm..." he moaned with his eyes closed.

I was bouncing all over his dick.

"Ahhh, it feels sooo good," I cried out, pressing my nails into his chest while his hands gripped my ass. I rocked back and forth on his dick and screamed his name repeatedly. I could tell by the look on his face that I was satisfying my man with every position.

"Pop that pussy for daddy."

He slapped my ass a few times which brought tears to my eyes. Sweat dripped from my body as my juices covered his dick. He lifted me up with both hands as he gripped my waist. He stroked the fucking life out of me.

"I'm cumming! I'm cumming!" I yelled out.

He didn't stop stroking my pussy. Instead, he sped up until he shot a load of his cum inside of me. He and I both lay there and stared into each other's eyes. As his body wrapped around my mine, I knew I had made the right decision by coming back home

# Chapter 6

## Zykiah

When Monica texted me last night and told me she was going back home, the news saddened me. I just hoped she was making the right decision. It all kind of worked out perfectly because Aubrey also hit me up, letting me know he was coming into town. I stepped into the kitchen in search of two wine glasses, but then I remembered the last time I used them was with Dewayne. I headed out toward the garage where I saw a box with *Glasses* written in bold letters. I opened it and grabbed two flutes.

It had been a while since I last used them. I blew the dust off them, and as I was leaving the garage, a picture of me and Wayne fell from an old Winchester clock. We were posted up against an old Chevy truck.

"Why couldn't you do right by me, Wayne?"

I picked up the old picture and placed it back on the clock. I smiled for a brief moment as I thought about the good times that we shared but then the thought of him and that other bitch rolled across my mind. That pretty smile quickly turned into a frown. I snapped back to reality fast. As soon as I reached the kitchen, I cleaned the dirty glasses and poured some Chianti, filling the glasses up halfway.

*KNOCK! KNOCK!*

*Who the fuck can this be?* I thought to myself while trying to see out of the peephole.

The only thing I saw was something dark because the person on the other end was blocking the hole.

"Who is it?" I asked aggressively

"It's me," the person behind the door replied.

"Who the fuck is me!" I yelled.

Now, whoever it was had really started to irritate me.

"Remove your damn finger before I grab my gun," I demanded.

When I looked this time, I saw who I had been expecting for weeks now. Finally, I opened the door. I ran into his arms and kissed him all over.

"Babe, I'm so happy to see you!"

I started kissing all over his bald head and face. Aubrey scooped me up and carried me into the house, closing the door behind us with his foot. When he put me down, I playfully hit him on his chest. He looked puzzled.

"That's for playing. I was about to grab my gun on your ass."

He just threw his hands up in surrender.

Aubrey was six feet five inches tall with a dark complexion and sexy as hell. His bald head complemented his neatly trimmed beard. He was wearing his favorite designer, Ralph Lauren. He had on a black shirt with a pair of Polo blue jeans and some classic black Timbs to complete the look.

Aubrey and I met on an online site, and we instantly vibed well with one another. When he and I actually talked on the phone, I knew he was the one. It was something about him that I was fascinated with. Still, to this day, I couldn't figure out why our chemistry was so strong.

“Come here,” I said with a seductive finger motion.

As soon as he came my way, our lips connected like two magnets. His hand squeezed my firm, juicy ass like no other. My eyes started rolling to the back of my head. His massive hands caressed my tight body. I dropped to my knees, pulled out his dick, and didn’t hesitate to lick the tip.

“Someone is happy to see me,” I said while sucking on the head of his dick.

“Shit!” he moaned, placing his hand on the back of my head.

I moved his hand and told him I had it. He looked down at me, licked his lips, and closed his eyes.

I spit on the head of his dick, used my hands to jack it, and popped it back into my mouth.

"Mmmm!" Aubrey cried out.

He was enjoying every second of the pleasure. I put his dick so far down my throat I gagged a little but not much because I was a pro. While I had his dick in my mouth, I massaged his balls with my free hand.

"Yes, babe, just like that! Damn, babe, suck this dick!" he cheered me on.

That had me moving faster and faster. My slippery wet mouth filled the air with slurping sounds. His dick was soaked. I had his toes curling up. He yanked me up because I put that mean head on him. A bitch was trying to put him out of commission. I spread my legs, and he dove right into my wet pussy and began to fuck me with his tongue.

He was hitting all the right spots. I was squirming all over the couch. He quickly grabbed my thighs to keep me in place. He didn't stop until he felt that white cream on his face.

"Mmm, daddy, eat this pussy!"

He then began sucking on my clit. My juices started

to squirt all the way to the ceiling. As I rubbed the top of my pussy, more came out. He just stood back and watched as I played with myself. After it was all over, I patted my pussy and signaled for him to come beat it up.

I climbed on the couch with my knees in the seat, and he slapped my fat ass cheeks. I reached back and parted my legs like the Red Sea. All that pussy was glowing in his face. Before he put his dick in, he gave it a kiss.

"Muah!"

I moaned as he slid inside of me and began to fuck me.

"Fuck this pussy, daddy!" I screamed out, moving fast on his dick.

"Shit, fuck me, babe," he moaned as he thrust harder, gripping my hair. That shit had my pussy about to overload.

"Daddy, I'm cumming! I'm cumming!" I screamed.

All the cum I had in me shot out. He didn't stop. That encouraged him to fuck me harder.

"Give me this pussy," he commanded as he choked me.

"Who pussy this is?"

"Yourrrrs!" I yelled out.

I was cumming all over again.

"Shit, baby! Cum in this pussy!" I moaned.

He thrust all the way in until I felt him in my stomach.

"I'm cumming!"

He released a great mass of nut inside me.

"I love you, Aubrey."

"I love you too, Kiah."

We lay in each other's arms looking at each other. We discussed all kind of shit until the fatigue got the best of us. We fell asleep for a little while only to get up in the middle of the night to start our freak show back up again.

# Chapter 7

## Monica

Zykiah and I were crushing the game today. She had on an all-white Fendi sundress that cupped her perfect B-cup breasts and hugged her nice round ass, white Fendi frames with *Fendi* written in red on the side, and a pair of Fendi sandals with red, diamond-studded straps. I was sporting my favorite white Prada shades with the gold trim. I had a white Prada t-shirt with the word D.R.A.K.E. It meant "Do It Right and Kill Everything," and I knew I was doing just that. I had on my white tennis skirt that showed off my tats and sexy legs and a pair of open-toe Prada flats. We were looking fabulous.

I started up the engine, and just as I was about to put the car into gear, Zykiah turned on J. Cole's CD *Cold World.* He was her favorite rapper.

"Damn! Mo, I love that light bright ass nigga!" Zykiah was screaming while trying to rap his song.

"Girl, you better sit your ass down," I replied.

"Don't shit get old but clothes. Shit, I could stand next to a twenty-year-old and take her man," she shot back and kept singing in my ear.

"Dolla and a dream, that's all a nigga got," she said, rapping and pointing her finger in the air.

Kiah was a beautiful woman at the age of thirty. Her skin was the creamiest black skin I'd ever seen. She had the perfect shape with the flattest stomach. You couldn't tell her anything. She knew she was fine. She had an attitude that came with it. I pulled into the parking space at a place called Ms. Bessie's. Ms. Bessie's was a country-style restaurant with an Italian swag. They served the most delicious food you ever tasted. The chemistry of the place was electrifying. People came from all over the world to come eat at Ms. Bessie's.

*I'm glad Ms. Bessie started her business in Albany,* I thought to myself as I tried finding me a spot to park. The parking lot was packed to the max with people lined up outside of the door trying to get in. The building had two stories. The first floor was just the buffet area, and the second floor was the dining area. I could smell the aroma of the food coming through the vents.

"Woah!" Zykiah said, snapping out of her singing.

"That food smells good," she said, smiling while rubbing her stomach.

"Yeah, Ms. Bessie's is the best spot in Albany," I responded.

"I heard about this place, but I never had time to come here," Kiah commented.

"C'mon, Kiah, I'mma show you how I get down."

We jumped out of the car. This was the perfect opportunity to spend time with my bestie. Once we entered the tall double doors, the aroma entered my nostrils. My feet just kept moving, following the smell of pork chops, ribs, fried chicken, and collard greens. The place was wall to wall with all types of people. Church people, bankers, street ballers, and some hoodrats were there too. We stepped inside, and the hostess showed us to our table.

The walls were covered with paintings of famous people such as Piero Della Francesca, Johannes Vermeer, and Martin Luther King. We sat under a portrait of Martin Luther King giving a speech.

I could see Zykiah's face. I could tell that the place amazed her. The spot was laid. It could have been a franchise easily, but Ms. Bessie just wanted to keep it in her hometown.

"This place is nice," Zykiah said and pointed at the picture of Michael Jordan flashing his rings.

"Yeah, Kiah, this place got me loving it. There's not a place like this anywhere else. I be wanting to come here every day, but I hate coming here alone because I hate to eat by myself," I said.

"Next time, just call me," she added.

"Yeah, right. You are too damn busy."

"Yeah, my new career be having me on the grind," she confessed.

"Yeah, I understand, Miss Book Writer," I teased.

"Don't do me like that!"

We burst out laughing and bobbed our heads to the classic music playing over the speaker. We talked amongst ourselves until our food was delivered to us. I ordered the smoked rib plate with a side of pasta salad. The Italian garlic bread that came with the salad would have you wanting to bite your fingers off. Zykiah was a virgin to this place. She kept it simple and had the country ham plate with a side of golden corn on the cob. We had a glass of Domaine Coche-Dury white wine.

"Mmm..." She took a sip of wine.

"That's good, huh?" I asked.

"Yes, boo!"

I was satisfied with the time I was spending with my bestie.

I glanced at Zykiah and just shook my head because she was throwing down. She was my rescue from my own reality. As I was enjoying myself, I felt someone watching me again. When I turned around, I saw this handsome guy waving at me, so I waved back. Zykiah gave me a nod to say, "I see you, girl." I just brushed her off because I wasn't into any other man.

"Mo, someone is coming this way," she said and smiled, showing her dimple.

Before I could respond, the guy was already at our table.

"Excuse me. I don't mean to be rude, but I can't help myself. You're the most beautiful woman I have ever seen," the man said flirtatiously.

Zykiah took it upon herself to introduce us because I was speechless.

"My name is Zykiah, and hers is Monica."

I gave her a look that said, "Girl, did you really have to give him my name too?"

I had to be honest. His words filled my confidence back up. I hadn't heard that in a while, but I couldn't break my vows to God for anyone, and Jihad and I had been doing good.

"Well, nice to meet you. My name is Marcus," he responded. He looked me dead in my eyes like I was his soulmate.

*Oh my God! This man is sexy,* I thought to myself.

"So, Mr. Marcus, what are you trying to get into?" Zykiah asked while kicking my foot under the table.

"To be honest, I would like to get to know your friend Monica," he said, never breaking eye contact with me.

"That would be nice."

His face lit up with happiness.

"But I'm a married woman," I emphasized and showed him the rock on my finger.

That stopped him in his tracks.

"I know he's a lucky man," he shot back.

Zykiah made a face like she was about to vomit.

"Glad to see that there are still women out there who are loyal."

"Yes, there are. I've been married for ten years," I said with a little neck.

"Nice to meet you anyway," he said then removed himself from our table and vanished into the crowd of people.

Zykiah had her face balled up.

"What?" I questioned her.

"*What?* Did you see how fine that nigga was?" she asked.

"Yeah, you forgot I'm a married woman," I said.

"Yeah, I kind of forgot about that lame," she said with a puppy dog expression.

She gulped some more wine from her glass. He was fine with his light-bright complexion, but at the end of the day, I couldn't risk my salvation for a cute smile. God would punish me dearly if I broke my promise to him. The waiter came with the check. I swiped the machine with my debit card and gave her a fifty-dollar tip for the service. I let Zykiah know I needed to go to the ladies' room. After I finished my personal business, I noticed an older woman beside me at the sink.

"How you doing, ma'am?" I greeted her.

"I'm doing fantastic!" she responded and asked how I was doing.

"I'm doing fine," I said, putting my head down.

"What's wrong?" the older lady asked with concern.

I hated that I could be read so easily.

My grandma told me a long time ago that older people have a gift of reading anybody like a book.

"Nun."

"C'mon, child. Don't be shy."

"Well, I've been in a marriage for ten years. Right now, we're building our relationship back up. I pray to God every day that it keeps going good," I confessed.

She looked at me then grabbed my hand. Her hands were so warm. She made me feel so relaxed. At that moment, she started saying a small prayer.

"Baby, I was married for thirty years before the good Lord called for Henry to come home to him.

We used to go back and forth as well, but the love we had for each other was impossible to break. When we felt like we had any issues, we made sure to talk them out. That's what's wrong with these people today; nobody wants to talk anymore," she preached to me, giving me a Godly hug.

"Thirty years is a long time," I said.

I wondered if Jihad and I were going to make it that long.

"Yes, baby, thirty years strong."

She just smiled at me. We went back and forth for a little while about our relationships. She gave me a card to one of her classes. She was a relationship expert. I knew Jihad would never want to go to anything like that. I let her know I would try to make it to one of her classes. We exchanged numbers, and I headed back to Zykiah. She looked confused like I had been abducted or something.

"'Bout damn time. I thought you got flushed down the toilet."

"Naw, I was talking to this older lady."

"I told you about talking to strangers!"

She burst out laughing and started squeezing my cheeks. The lady had me thinking hard about my marriage.

"Lord, are we gonna make it to see thirty years?" I asked myself.

We got into the car. I dropped that fool, Zykiah, off. Then, I was in the wind to my house.

# Chapter 8

## Monica

### A Week Later

Kiah and I had just come back in town from the Moody Theater in Austin, Texas. Kiah had a book signing, and Miranda Lambert was performing.

"I enjoyed Texas, girl," I said to Zykiah as I was pulling up to her condo.

"Yeah, that girl can sing her ass off, too," she said.

"I never was a fan of country, but the way she played that guitar made me become a fan."

We slapped each other's hand.

"I know my fingers hurt from signing all those books," she said, massaging her palm.

"I'm tired as well," I said, helping her gather her belongings.

I watched her until she disappeared into the house before I drove off to my home sweet home.

It took me approximately ten minutes to arrive at home. It'd been six months since me and Jihad reconciled. I even had him attending church every other

Sunday. When I pulled into my driveway, I was exhausted and ready to hit my bed. As I walked to the door, I heard the television blasting.

*Jihad must have company,* I thought to myself.

I opened the door. I got a bad vibe, but I brushed it off. I immediately turned the TV off because it was too loud.

"Jihad, are you here!" I yelled throughout the house.

Glancing around my home, it looked like Jihad had a huge party. Liquor bottles were everywhere. It smelled awful.

"Nooo. My babies!" I screamed as I grabbed my flower vase. I was heated. Jihad had destroyed my damn flowers.

"How?" I kept repeating to myself.

Tears were building up because I'd spent hours grooming those flowers.

"Jihad!" I screamed as I stormed upstairs.

When I opened my bedroom door, I thought my eyes were playing tricks on me. It was unbelievable. I lost it. I dashed to the hallway closet. I grabbed the .45 that Zykiah gave me for my birthday the year before and headed back to my room. Jihad was enjoying himself so good that he didn't see me come in.

"Jihad!" I yelled.

He nearly jumped out of the window. The little hoe he had sucking his dick jumped up, grabbed the sheets, and screamed.

"Mo, babe," he pleaded with his hands up.

Tears were pouring out of my eyes. My heart was pounding.

"Don't fucking *Mo* me, motherfucker!" I barked and aimed the gun at both low-life motherfuckers.

"Let me explain."

"Explain what? She slipped on yo' dick?" I said aggressively.

"Ba—" I cut him off immediately.

"Shut the fuck up, Jihad. All I've done for you... nigga, fuck you! Now, I'm gonna show you my fucking payback! It's finna be bigger than you can imagine, motherfucker."

I pulled the trigger. A bullet hit Jihad in the chest. His body hit the floor. Blood erupted from his chest.

"Uh…uh…" Jihad was trying to catch his breath.

I just stood over him, looking him in his eyes.

"You chose this life," I said, pulling the trigger again, putting one directly in his fucking head and giving him something to think about. The bloodshot upwards, hitting me in the face. I was on fire. There was no turning back now.

"Mmm... Please, don't kill me," the little bitch said in the corner, crying for her dear life.

I looked her dead in her eyes and blasted the shit out of her. Her brain matter splattered all over the walls. I couldn't take it anymore; it was too much. I put the gun to my temple. I didn't want to live anymore.

*CLICK! CLICK!*

The room started spinning. I kept pulling the trigger, but nothing was coming out. I fell to my knees and cried.

"Why me, God!" I screamed, looking at the ceiling.

Tears covered my entire face. I grabbed a lamp and threw it against the wall. I made the mirror on the wall hit the floor. I sat there on the floor looking at their lifeless bodies. I didn't understand life. I grabbed my phone to call the only person I knew could help me and calm me down.

"Sup, Mo?"

Silence.

"Mo, you okay? Say something."

"Kiah... I..."

It was too overwhelming for me. This couldn't be happening. I just cried on the phone.

"Mo! Mo!"

"He gone, Kiah."

"Who, Mo?"

"Kiah, I shot him."

"I'll be there in ten minutes."

In exactly ten minutes, she was knocking on my door. When I opened the door, she embraced me. She didn't care how bloody my clothes were.

"It's going to be okay, Mo. I'm here for you."

"I don't want to go to prison!" I cried out, thinking about wearing a jumpsuit.

I buried my face in her chest. She grabbed my shoulder.

"Look, get it together," she demanded.

I wiped the tears from my eyes.

"It's not the time to be soft right now. We're going to get through this," she said, pulling out her phone.

*KNOCK! KNOCK!* My whole body jerked because I thought it was all over for me.

Zykiah told me to calm down. She opened the door, and a tall nigga who was caramel in complexion appeared out of the dark.

"This my cuz, Ja'Noah. Ja'Noah, this Monica," Zykiah introduced us.

I was lost.

He nodded his head at me before turning toward Kiah.

"He's here to get rid of the bodies," she informed me. I was at a loss for words.

"Show me where they're at," Ja'Noah said.

When I opened the bedroom door, it played back in my head. I glanced at Zykiah. Her face showed that she was in total shock.

"Damn, Mo, you that bitch," she said.

"Kiah, this is too much."

"Go clean yourself up. We got this," she commanded.

I did what I was told and headed to the bathroom. I filled the tub with some coconut body wash and soaked in the warm water. It really relieved some of the tension that I had in my body. When I got out the tub, I threw on a plain white Mickey Mouse shirt and some black leggings.

After I was dressed, I headed to my bedroom where I noticed that Jihad and the bitch were gone. My heart felt as if it had been stabbed multiple times as tears fell down my cheeks. The room smelled of bleach and other cleaning products, but everything looked to be clean and in order. Kiah had even changed the bed sheets for me. I was grateful for her.

I headed toward the living room where I saw Kiah

waiting for me. She had a crazy smirk on her face.

"Where Ja'Noah at?" I asked.

"He's gone to handle his business. Look, Mo, this is what you got to do."

I gave her my full attention.

"Mo, you have to call the police."

"What? No!" I yelled. My palms began to sweat. My nerves were running wild.

"Bitch, calm down," she said, shaking my shoulders and looking me in my eyes.

"You gotta file a missing person's report. That way, you'll have something on record."

Her words made sense, but I still didn't want to do it.

"You think that's gonna work?" I asked.

"Yes, it's going to work."

"I don't know, Kiah," I said. I was scared to death.

"Just trust me," she said with a gentle pat on my thigh. I took her advice.

"Okay, I'm gonna do it, but I need to be alone. I got to get my thoughts together."

I headed downstairs, sat on the couch, and got comfortable. I inhaled then exhaled before I dialed the three-digit number.

"What's your emergency?"

“Yes, I wanted to report that my husband is missing, I cried into the phone.

“Ma’am, what is the missing person’s name?” she asked calmly.

“Jihad Johntavious Carter.”

“Excuse me, did you just say Jihad Carter?” she asked like she was shocked.

“Yes, that’s my husband’s name. Is something wrong?” I questioned.

“Sorry about that. It’s just... I see his picture on the billboard on my way to work every day,” she said.

She wrote my information down and told me to come in the morning so I could talk to someone.

I was glad that session was over with. I hopped up when I noticed that Kiah was coming with a big trash bag. I went to assist her because she looked like she was struggling.

“Geez, I’m tired, bitch,” she said as she wiped the sweat from her forehead.

“I’m truly thankful to have you.”

“You owe me, bitch,” she joked.

“I got you.”

I gave her a huge hug and made sure she got in her car safely. I waved goodbye as I threw the heavy trash bag in the trash can outside. I closed the door behind me and laid on the couch until I finally dozed off into a deep sleep.

# Chapter 9

## Monica

### Three Days Later

*RING! RING!*

That's all I heard coming from out of nowhere. *Who could be calling me this early in the morning?* The phone was jumping off the hook. *Where is my phone at?* I tossed the huge blanket left and right trying to find it. My head was pounding with pain. I had a hangover out of this world. I had been drinking for the past three days. My mouth was super dry.

"Hello?"

"Turn to the news on ASAP."

I turned to the local news. I saw a reporter talking about two bodies that had been discovered. I repositioned myself and turned the volume up to the max. That's when Jihad's picture appeared on the screen along with his little bitch. The reporter said that Jihad had been brutally murdered. She went ahead to describe the gunshot wounds. The bodies were found late last night by a truck driver in Houston, Texas.

"Texas. That's a little ride from Georgia to Texas," I said to myself.

The reporter said that they had no suspects at the moment. The detective came on and said there would be a full investigation. The camera zoomed in on his lips.

"We will find you," the detective stated.

It felt like he was talking to me. I turned the TV completely off.

"You ok, Mo?" Zykiah asked.

"Yeah, I just feel weird about it."

"I know how you feel, boo. Remember Dewayne?"

"Yeah."

"You know what happened to him?"

"You told me he skipped town, bitch."

Kiah rolled her eyes.

"Bitch, you know that nigga didn't skip no town. I killed his ass. I was sick and tired of the cheating, so I had to put that nigga six feet deep."

I'm not going to lie, Kiah was a crazy bitch who knew a lot of people that could make a nigga disappear. I figured Wayne was dead somewhere, but I kept my mouth closed because I didn't want to know the truth.

Kiah tried to warn me about Jihad, but I wouldn't listen to her. Now, I was feeling dumb as hell because I had committed two murders.

*KNOCK! KNOCK!*

"Hold on. Someone is at the door."

"Who?"

"I don't know."

Before I opened the door, I looked out the peephole. I saw a badge.

"Albany police! Anyone here?"

"Kiah, I'm going to have to call you back."

After I had disconnected the call, I opened the door, and I saw a white woman dressed in a black shirt and khaki pants. She was five feet five with long sandy hair. She was not ugly nor pretty; she was just average.

"Good morning. May I help you?"

I greeted her with a weird frown because her perfume had my nostrils on fire.

"Yes, you may." She flashed her badge.

"I'm detective Amber McDonald, and this is Detective Rolle. We are here to ask you a few questions concerning your husband."

My heart was about to jump out of my chest and into my hands. *They don't know it was me,* I told myself. *I won't break or let them read me. I refuse to spend the rest of my life behind those prison walls.*

"Monica, calm down. Get yourself together," my inner voice kept saying to me.

I looked over at Detective McDonald's partner, and my heart began to race. Little did she know, this was not my first encounter with Detective Rolle, aka Marcus. He extended his hand, and I extended mine back to give him a proper greeting.

They both headed to my living room, took a seat on my couch, and took their notepads out.

Detective McDonald didn't waste any time getting to the point. She scanned the house. I hadn't the slightest idea what she is looking for. She repositioned herself on the couch. I knew she was about to drop a series of questions on me.

"First off, I'd like to say I'm sorry about the loss of your husband." She grabbed my hand. It felt sincere, but I still didn't trust her ass. "I just want to ask you a few questions, and we will be out the way."

I nodded my head as I took a seat and waited.

"Please state your name."

"Monica Dashika Carter," I responded.

"Thanks."

I just nodded my head.

"When was the last time you saw or talked to Jihad?"

she asked.

"Early Monday morning... before I left the house."

I tried to stay focused on her question, but Marcus was looking me dead in my eyes. The fact that he was so damn sexy was distracting me.

"So, Monday was the last time you talked to him?" I nodded my head.

She wrote more on the pad.

"Did your husband have any close friends?"

"Not really. The only friends he had were the ones he dealt with on his business trips."

"Right now, we have no suspects, but my units are working overtime to crack this case."

I didn't respond because I was ready for them to leave my house.

"What kind of business did he have in Texas?" she asked.

"I have no earthly idea about his business. Only thing I did was take care of the house. I knew about the limousine company because that was my idea," I explained to her.

She had me nervous because she kept with the questions. The demon inside me told me to go in the safe, grab Jihad's gun, and come back and shoot both of them.

I knew that would only make matters worse, so I just sat there and listened to her.

"Detective McDonald, let me speak with Ms—"

"Mrs. Carter," I cut him off.

I was kind of glad he jumped in because I wanted to slap his partner. He must have sensed the vibe we were giving each other. She did what she was told but didn't take her eyes off me. I kept watching her. For some reason, I didn't feel that she believed me. After a few moments of trying to ask me questions, the tension was thick in the room. He looked over at his partner and whispered something in her ear before she got up and walked out the house.

"I sent her to the car, so try to relax for me."

"Well, Mrs. Carter, I just want to say that you're more beautiful than before," Marcus said before sliding closer to me.

"Thank you, but aren't you supposed to be asking me questions about my husband?" I scooted to the far end.

"I am, but she asked you all the questions we needed answers to. But I do have one last question? Did you have anything to do with your husband being murdered?"

My heart sunk into my lap. *I know this fool didn't just ask me that.* I was heated now and was ten seconds away from punching his ass Sometimes people can do too much.

"Of course not," I shot back. My whole demeanor changed. "Well, if there ain't any more questions, then I think it's time for you to leave," I expressed, walking him to the door.

"Here is my card." He handed it to me on his way out the door. I glanced at it.

*Detective Marcus Rolle*

*Phone: 555-485-6734*

I closed the door behind him, threw the card in my purse, and headed to the bathroom so I could take a shower.

# Chapter 10

## Monica

Pulling up at Yaz, it was very difficult finding a parking spot. I finally found one next to a dusty white minivan. From the looks of it, there were some kids in the back of it. It was sizzling hot outside, and I was close to pulling my phone out and calling the police, but I had a lot of shit going on, so I said fuck it.

As I threw the car in park, I heard my phone ring. I knew it was Zykiah calling or texting because I heard Rihanna's "BBHMM" playing.

**Kiah:** *You okay, boo?*

The text scrolled across the screen.

**Me:** *Yea*

I replied with smiley faces.

**Kiah:** *Wyd hunni?*

**Me:** *Bout to walk in Yaz and get a change up, and u?*

This time she didn't respond as fast, so I grabbed all my belongings and headed to the front entrance. As soon as I hit the alarm, I noticed begging ass Flo coming toward me. I tried to hurry my ass up and prayed she didn't see me. Before I could let the prayer leave my mind, she was on me like white on rice.

"Hey, Monica, how are you doing?" Flo asked, trying to get me to hug her.

I was not trying to get involved with her shit. It was too hot to be bothered.

"I'm gucci," I said, pushing right past her, but she was on my heels.

"Sorry for the loss of Jihad."

I just stared at her and gave her a fake smile. I had a lot on my mind. I couldn't even think clearly, so I said thanks and pushed on. I opened the door and watched it close in her face as she was standing there looking dumb. Soon as I stepped foot in the shop, I threw my hand up and waved to this old-school lady named Ms. McKenzie. She had been in the first booth since day one. She was the real reason for Yaz's success. The place was packed with teenagers talking about who was going to take them to the prom. Then, in the corner, you had the lowlife hoodrat bitches that gossiped about everybody's business. I just smiled at them because if they wanted to get wrong, I was going to give them something to talk about. I strolled to the back to see what Yaz was up to.

"Hey, Yaz!" I crept up behind her.

She turned around and beamed.

"Heyyy, girl!" She was so excited to see me she dropped the curlers and combs and hugged my neck tightly. I felt I wasn't able to breathe. The other females looked at us like we were crazy. She gave me a small kiss on the cheek and whispered in my ear that everything was going to be okay.

I just said thanks because I didn't have many words to say about the situation. I let her get back to her client.

"Yaz, how many you got because I need a good do?" I asked as I began taking my hair down.

"I have one more in front of you."

"Okay, cool."

I pulled a small chair in her section then pulled out my iPhone. I was about to hit up Facebook until I realized I was texting Kiah before I stepped into the shop.

**Kiah**: *Bout to have some freaky sex.*

She sent that with smiley faces. I read the other one.

**Kiah:** *You still there?*

I let her know she was nasty and that I needed to talk to her about something I had been thinking about for the past couple of days. My phone kept vibrating, letting me know about the notifications I had on Facebook. I jumped on Facebook to check my inbox. I had so many messages saying, "Sorry to hear about Jihad." I responded to mostly my cousins, uncles, and aunties because the rest were nobodies.

Somebody felt like I wanted all the pictures Jihad and I all over my page because I was constantly getting tagged in shit. Every time I saw a picture of him, my veins pumped with hatred for him taking advantage of me for all these years. After all, I had done for him, he gave me no respect in return. I sacrificed a lot for that motherfucker.

"God, you let me down. That will never happen again because from now on, I'm controlling my own destiny."

I sat there reminiscing about the time I gave Jihad my virginity.

*It was one day after high school. Jihad invited me back to his house. We were so in love that "No" was not in our vocabulary. I knew it was okay because Jihad's parents were never there. They were either at work, or they were always taking long ass vacations and leaving him with the nanny. Before he opened the door, he looked me in my eyes. My whole body froze up then melted. I tried to turn my head, but he grabbed my chin and inserted his tongue into my mouth. My tongue moved with his. As we kissed, he led me to his room and closed his door behind us. Everything was perfect, just like one of those love movies that I used to love to watch. We made it to the bed, and we were going at it like wild animals. I pushed him up because I felt my panties getting moist, and I started to become nervous.*

*"Do you really love me?" I asked him.*

*"I love you with all of my heart. The only thing I see in the future is you. I will never hurt you, baby," he said, placing kisses all over my face.*

*That's all I wanted to hear. I was ready to give him my goodies.*

*His body language was joyful; he had been waiting for this moment.*

*"Are you ready for this?"*

*I didn't respond.*

*Instead, I took his shirt off to let him know I was for real. We undressed each other. He tried to put a condom on, but I told him no because I wanted to feel the real thing. He penetrated me with his dick, and I squinted my eyes, trying to endure the pain. The pain shot up my spine, and my whole body was numb.*

*He went back and forth as he held on to me. It hurt, but I was too far in now to turn back. He was gentle and kept checking on me by asking if I were okay. I had my eyes closed the whole time, biting my bottom lip. He kept telling me to cum for him. I didn't know how because I'd never done it before. His thrusts increased. He went faster and faster.*

*Now, it was starting to get better. The top of my pussy was jumping repeatedly. I moaned out. Once I did that, it seemed like I turned him on, so I kept doing it. He had me at a place I couldn't imagine or speak of. My legs started shaking, and I grabbed him tightly. I could feel this creamy liquid come out of me, and my energy was gone. I felt lighter than a feather. I was on cloud nine, and I was deeply in love with the man who had made me a woman.*

"Mo!" Yaz snapped me back to reality, letting me know I was next. I grabbed my purse and jumped in the chair. Some of the hoodrats got mad because they had been sitting there all morning. I informed her that there were kids outside in a hot car.

"Attention! If you left your kids in the car, you dead ass wrong!" Yaz announced.

One of the hoodrats in the corner stood up and walked outside to get her kids. Yaz and I shook our heads.

"What you getting?" she asked me, running her

fingers through my hair.

"Well, I want a different look."

I really didn't know what I wanted. I scanned the room and pointed at this woman who was rocking a short bob.

"I want my hair like that," I said as I pointed at the woman. She just looked at me like I had lost my mind. She grabbed my long hair and ran her hands through it again. I always used to refuse to let her cut my hair, but today was different. I wanted a new look. I gave her the thumbs up.

"You crazy!" Yaz replied, but she grabbed her tools and went to work. She washed it and even put a little color in it. Before I knew it, she was done.

"Wow, you look beautiful," Yaz said, spinning the chair around so I could view myself in the wall mirror.

As I opened my eyes, the entire salon was looking at me. When I saw myself, it was some outstanding work she had done.

"Thanks, Yaz!" I hugged her neck tightly.

"No problem, looking like Rihanna."

I took my phone out and took a selfie of Yaz and I and posted it on Facebook with the caption *New life, new look!*

I texted Kiah back and told her to meet me at the crib later that night. I said my goodbyes to Yaz just before I reached in my pursed and thumbed through the stack of money I had inside. I grabbed three crispy one hundred-dollar bills, folded them up, and handed them to Yaz. She looked in amazement. I just waved goodbye again and pushed on.

I jumped in my Maserati Quattroporte and went about my business. I stopped at the mall to load up on some gear. After I left the mall, I stopped by Cold Stone to grab some ice cream. I had a chocolate waffle cone with strawberry cheesecake flavored ice cream.

I sat in the park and enjoyed my ice cream, as I did a little thinking about my future. It's funny how men thought that they were untouchable because they had money. My phone vibrated to let me know that I had a text message. I smiled when I saw that it was Kiah, and she agreed that we would meet up tonight. When she started texting me about some nigga she had met, I couldn't help but laugh. She explained how the sex wasn't hitting on shit. I read the rest of it and laughed like hell at the crazy ass fool. As I was about to push start to get out of there, I heard a pecking knock on the window. It was a church lady named Ms. Betty.

"Hey, Ms. Betty," I greeted her while rolling down the window.

"Monica, how you been?" she asked me, giving me a small kiss on the cheek.

"I been maintaining."

"Why you ain't been at church? We miss you."

"I just have a lot on my plate."

"I understand, baby, but no matter what's going on, just give it to God," she suggested.

"I know. I'll think about this Sunday," I lied, but if that got her to stop preaching, I was going with it. Her grandkids were calling her, so she told me that she would see me in church Sunday.

Ms. Betty was a sixty-year-old that raised four generations of kids—ten doctors, two policemen, and five preachers with huge churches. Her track record of teaching was amazing. She was respected in the community and was the reason the kids came to church. When I was growing up, she used to load us up in her station wagon and take us back if you didn't have a way. She always preached to me about street life and said it's nothing but hardship.

Deep down, I was not into the church life right now. God and I had a lot to talk about, but it was time that I did my own thing. I started up my whip and popped in Plies' *Real Testament*, hit track fifteen "Murder Season," and zoomed through traffic.

# Chapter 11

## Monica

As I sat in my house, so many memories flashed in my head. The phrase "Home Sweet Home" was a lie because I was never happy here. He hit me in my mouth for the first time in the kitchen because I questioned him about his whereabouts for coming in at 2:00 a.m. He said when I started paying bills, that's when I could question him. I stayed in the house several days so the bruises could clear up.

The next day, he brought me a brand-new Chanel bag. I was not a materialistic person. I prayed extra hard for our marriage. He was cool for a couple more weeks. Then, one day in the living room, he just snapped. After the fight was over, I had a broken rib. To top it all off, the selfish motherfucker didn't come check on me. All the pain and suffering I endured over him had me joyful that I put holes in him. His love had killed me on the inside.

When I saw a light shine through my blinds, I jumped up and opened the door. Kiah had the music blasting. I stood in the doorway looking at her stupid ass trying to rap. She cut off her car, jumped out, and ran my way. We hugged each other and gave each other a girly kiss on the forehead.

"Damn, bitch, really?" she said with a perplexed look on her face, running her fingers through my hair.

"You like it?" I asked as I was doing different poses against the wall.

"Hell yeah! You're so beautiful, Mo! You know if your grandma was still living, she would kill you."

I agreed with her because my beloved granny would've been crushed and would've wanted to kill me for cutting my beautiful hair. She used to always tell me that I had pretty, long black hair. She was so hard on me growing up. I guess the fact that my mom wasn't stable enough to take care of me she took it upon herself to be my parent.

One day after school, I didn't come straight home. I took a detour to my classmate's house to let her put a perm in my head. I didn't know what to expect when I stepped into Shamaria's house that day.

*"Just sit right here," Shamaria instructed me, sitting on a small wooden chair. Shamaria was a grade higher than me, so I felt a little comfortable with her. Shamaria did mostly everyone's hair in the neighborhood. She wrapped an apron around me, combing my hair to the*

*back. The scent of the chemicals had my nostrils burning.*

*"Why do it smell like that?" I asked while holding my nose together.*

*"I don't know, but first it will be cold and then it will warm up," she said, applying the thick, creamy formula to my hair. It sat on my hair for a good five minutes and nothing happened. Suddenly, my skull felt like a torch hit it. I know how Michael Jackson felt on that Pepsi commercial.*

*"Is it supposed to be burning?" I asked out of concern. I couldn't take anymore, but I was not a coward.*

*"Yeah, the more it burns, the better," she added. I endured the pain just for a little while longer. After five minutes, she rinsed it out. While she was washing it out, I saw my hair floating in the sink. I reached into my head, and my hair was coming out in clumps.*

*"I'm so sorry!" she apologized. I didn't know what to do. When I made it home, my granny was waiting at the door. She noticed the patch. I tried to explain what happened. Granny beat me every day until that patch filled back in. She told me to never let anybody play in my hair.*

My grandma was probably turning over in her grave at this very moment, but it didn't matter. I loved my new look. It was time for a change.

Kiah looked around my place and pointed to the packed boxes that were sitting on the living room floor. That's when I told her that I could no longer live in this house. There were way too many bad memories to continue to live here. After I told her about the new apartment that I had just leased, we headed toward the kitchen and took a seat.

"I need to talk to you about something."

I looked into her eyes to let her know that I was being serious.

"Wassup, Mo?"

I stood up and grabbed my bottle of wine out of the fridge and poured me a glass before I took a seat and cleared my throat.

"I've been thinking about a lot of things."

"Like what?" she responded.

I instructed her to come back to sit down so I could have her full attention. I needed her to be ready for what I was about to hit her with.

"I was a damn good woman to Jihad."

She remained silent and nodded her head.

"I put up with shit that most women wouldn't even put up with. Now, I'm at my last straw."

"What are you saying, Mo?" she inquired.

"After all the shit I've been through, it's time for fucking payback, and I mean  big fucking payback. I'm going to be the voice for all the silent, abused women out there. I want to regain terror on the men who think they can't be touched and believes the world revolves around them. I know you know people Kiah. So I was hoping that you could get me in contact with the right people."

No longer was I going to wait on God to solve my problems instead I wanted to take matters into my own hands. I was ready to stand up for the women who weren't able to do it themselves. I was ready to murk every nigga that was doing some fucked up shit. Every man that mistreated their spouse would feel my wrath and madness. I would slay all their asses and drink me a glass of wine afterward.

We drank for the rest of the night. We started off playing cards while watching different old school movies like *Waiting to Exhale, The Wood,* and *Three Deadly Words.* I enjoyed her presence because I needed to vent to her. We talked until our eyes got heavy.

A Few Days Later

On the day of the funeral, it was packed like the

Million Man March. People I had never seen before were even present. I had just pulled up at the church and stepped out of the car when I spotted some of Jihad's fake ass people coming my way.

"Hey, Mo! How are you?" Jihad's cousin, KeKe, greeted me with a half hug.

She and I were never the best of in-laws. She was the type of person that never had a stable living situation. We basically paid all her bills while she stayed in the House of Jazz all night looking for her next fix or young hustler to sell herself to. Now, she's going to be looking crazy because I don't give a flying fuck about her stank ass. The only person I did love on his side was his niece, Tyra. She was the prettiest child I had ever seen. She was only ten years old and had the voice of Anita Baker in her prime.

"Hey, Baby," I greeted Tyra with a motherly hug.

I looked back at KeKe and noticed she was still waiting for me to respond.

"I've been doing fine. Just trying to make it the best way I know how."

"Well, if you need anything, let me know. I'm here for you."

I looked at her for a brief moment and was close to

laughing in her face because that bitch was higher than a kite. I cringed when she gave Tyra a hug and walked away. Tyra fell head first to my chest sniffling. Tears were falling on my dress.

"Why they had to do him like that?" Tyra cried to me.

"I don't know, baby."

I felt guilty as hell as I lied to her. I just held her tighter against me. It was a very awkward moment. I felt so low. My mind replayed all the times he used to slap me for no reason.

I gave her some tissue to clean her face up. The funeral dictator showed us the way into the church. As we entered the temple of the Lord, the music played. The choir sang "Take Me to the King." My nerves went haywire seeing all those people in there. I walked closer to the casket surrounded by pictures of Jihad throughout his life. As I got closer to his casket, an usher came to me and asked me if I was going to be okay. I gestured with my hands to let her know I was good. I placed my hand on the casket, and all I could hear was Jihad's voice circling in my head, telling me that I wasn't shit. The flashback was getting clearer and clearer. It made me smirk even harder. I wish I could've put him in the ground a long time ago. All eyes were on me as I bent my head down in the casket as if I were kissing him. My lips didn't meet his cheek. Instead, I whispered in his ear and told him to burn in hell. After I was done, I took my seat in the front row.

"It's going to be okay," one of Jihads cousins told me as she handed me some tissue. If only she knew those tears were for joy. I was not vulnerable, weak ass Monica anymore. This was the new and improved Monica. I was on that Steve Harvey mantra, "If you don't like me, I don't like you." I sat next to his aunt, Sue Mae. We exchanged words, but I knew she wasn't a big fan of mine. They didn't like me because they felt like I thought I was better than them. I treated all his people with Godly love up until this point. I didn't really care. I just gave her a fake smile too.

As I looked around the church to see how crowded it was, I noticed a young boy who was standing beside the casket, peeking in. He looked like the spitting image of Jihad. My heart turned from red to charcoal black. The young boy stood there with an older lady, who I assumed was his grandmother. The child was crying hysterically, calling out, "Daddy!" and reaching for his pictures. That had my insides boiling. As I looked to the right, KeKe stared at me with a smirk on her damn face. I wanted to wrap my hands around that bitch's throat and murder her ass. Instead, I turned the other way and forced the tears to not fall from my eyes. I was angry and hurt. This nigga had a child that I didn't even know about. *Damn,* I thought to myself. *I probably never would have known either.* I was glad that nigga was dead.

The usher escorted the older lady and the child to their seats. I knew that the funeral was about to start. Bishop Johnson made a gesture for the whole congregation to stand up.

"We are gathered here today for the homecoming of Mr. Jihad Johntavious Carter. See, Mr. Carter was a good man in the community…" Everyone clapped and screamed their "Amens." I just wished he would hurry up because they didn't really know Jihad.

"Jihad will leave his wife behind."

He pointed in my direction, and I held my silk handkerchief to my face. The Bishop went on and on about how good he was. A couple of his close friends got up and spoke. I hadn't seen them in years. After each one was done, they stopped by and gave me a hug. Some left their cards and told me if I needed anybody to talk to, to hit them up.

"You ok, Mrs. Carter?" A church member came with

some tissue.

I didn't respond; I just nodded my head. I could've won an Oscar for my performance. When it was all over, I scanned the churchyard for my car. On my way to my car, I saw the old lady and the child leave.

They were riding in a black and silver Mercedes Benz GLC coupe. I wondered what she did to be able to afford that car. I wondered, but I already knew that Jihad probably had something to do with all that. Instead of dwelling on what other secrets that Jihad probably had, I hopped in my car and headed back home.

# Chapter 12

## Monica

*RING! RING!*

I kept hearing the phone ring. I didn't want to answer it, but the ringing was becoming annoying as hell. As I rolled over, I noticed the clock displayed 8:00 a.m. Now, I was really a pissed off motherfucker.

"Yeah!" I yelled into the phone.

"Good morning, Mrs. Carter, how are you?" the guy on the other end asked.

"May I ask whom I'm speaking with?" I asked rudely.

The phone got silent, so I started pushing numbers because I was about to hit the end button. For once, I was sleeping damn good and was angry that it was interrupted.

"This is Detective Rolle."

My heart started pounding hard, and my palms got moist. *They have caught me.* My nerves started running me up the wall. I closed my eyes, and all I could see was an image of me wearing a prison outfit.

"I know you're going through a lot right now. I don't

want to sound disrespectful, but I just want to take you out to dinner," he said.

My heart and my mind slowed down. Thank God that moment was over. I thought he was about to tell me it was over with.

"To be honest, I don't know if that's a good idea."

"Just think about it. I've been going to Ms. Bessie's every day anticipating you showing up."

"Really?" I shot back.

"I can't stop thinking about you," he confessed.

He had me blushing.

Marcus continued talking about how much he was feeling me and how he was going to treat me like a queen. That's the same ole line every man used to try to advertise with. I soaked in his words and the more I was trying not to hear his charm, his words were still out of this world. Instead of telling him I would let him take me out, I told him I would get at him later. I saved his number, and I dialed Kiah's number.

"Heyyy, boo!" Kiah greeted me, blowing kisses in the phone.

"Wassup, girl?" I responded.

"Shit, just waking up."

"Wassup with that lil' business we discussed?" I got

straight to the point. My trigger finger had been itching.

The demon had woken up. I was ready to send these other ungrateful niggas to fucking hell.

"Yeah, I put you in line with it. Did you receive the text yet?"

"Nawl, not yet."

A ding on my phone alerted me that I had a message.

"Hold on, Kiah. I just got a text."

When I opened it up, I noticed the text was from a weird ass number.

"Let me hit you back later, Kiah. I just got the information."

"Just be careful, Mo!"

I assured her that I would, and we hung up our phones. I read through the text messages as they began to flood my phone. It didn't take long before I got the rules. I agreed to all the terms, and that was it. Within seconds, pictures started coming through the phone. There was a catalog of men. I was astonished when I saw who was first on the list. When I saw Bishop Johnson's name and picture, I was in utter shock. He stood in the pulpit every Sunday preaching to people about doing God's work, and he was living in sin himself. I'll deal with him later. Until then, I was ready to choose my first man.

I scrolled down the list and clicked on Mr. Samual Harris' picture. He was the CEO of Bank of America. I copied the address down and decided that he was going to be the first on my list. After I was done viewing all the men that were sent to my phone, I slid out of bed and headed toward the bathroom so I could take a hot bath. I filled the tub up with some Victoria's Secret Cucumber Melon bubble bath, slid into the tub, closed my eyes, and listened to some Xscape. After I was done with my bath, I stepped out, dried my body off, and began to get dressed for the day.

## A Few Days Later

At 6:00 a.m., I pulled up a block down from the home of Samual Harris. The wind was blowing hard. As I shut off the Porsche Cayenne, I slid my hands into some black leather gloves so I wouldn't leave any fingerprints. I had been watching the house for a couple of days now, so I knew his neighbors' whereabouts day in and day out. As I crept behind the Jeep Grand Cherokee, I crouched down on the moist grass. I crept along the side until I made it to the garage where his sky-blue Bentley Continental GT was parked. I pulled out the spare key I had made earlier in the week when I tricked the locksmith into unlocking the door. I turned the handle and proceeded in. I knew he would be starting his day bright and early, so I had to hurry before he caught me slipping. As I entered the living room area, the strawberry scent entered my nostrils. I noticed a small device spraying every few seconds.

I pulled my gun out and made sure that my silencer was intact. I grabbed my phone out of my pocket so I could see the layout of his house one last time. I needed to go upstairs, make a right at the second door, and the man of the house would be there. The staircase had about fifteen steps, but the way I was up them it seemed like two.

The first room's door was a little ajar, so I peeped my head in and saw a curved, sixty-two-inch plasma TV with different video games laying around.

*This must have been his man cave,* I thought to myself.

As I came upon the room, I could hear loud snoring. I pushed the door open slowly. It made a slight sound, but he was out of it and didn't stop snoring to wake up. I pulled the sheets back. He was sleeping like a baby with nothing on but his boxers. I shook my head and put the cold silencer to his forehead.

"Wake up!" The rage in my voice surprised him.

He jumped up in shock when he realized he had a gun to his dome. Reality kicked in.

"Don't kill me!" he begged for his life like I gave a damn about it.

He knew his time was coming to an end. Our eyes locked. I had so much hate in mine.

"I'll give you whatever you want!" He was still trying to bargain for his life.

"Anything I want?" I toyed with him.

He nodded his head rapidly.

"I want your life."

I pulled the trigger so fast his brain matter spattered all over the headboard, and his limp body fell to the floor. I glanced at the nightstand on my way out the door. I saw a picture of him and his kids at the park. I didn't shed a tear as I ran back toward my car.

As I started my car, I noticed someone was watching me. I didn't sweat it too much. I was gone in the wind within six seconds. Ten minutes later, I was pulling back up at my apartment when my phone began to blast Travis Scott. I opened the text message and was shocked to see that my money had already been delivered to me. When I stepped out of my car, a few of my neighbors were leaving their house for work and tried speaking to me, but I gave them a look to leave me the hell alone.

Once my feet touched the pearl-white carpet, I knew I was home sweet home. I was relieved. I headed toward my bedroom, and that's when I noticed the manila envelope laying on my bed. I counted the money and was shocked to learn that it was close to $30,000. I messaged Kiah and told her I was going to give her ten out of it because she put me on.

I stripped naked and hopped in the shower. Things were looking good for me. I was finally happy again.

# Chapter 13

## Monica

The morning sun peered through the blinds. It hit every angle of my scrumptious masterpiece of a body. I slid out of bed and took a look around my house. It needed cleaning, so after I fixed me a nice breakfast, I decided it was time to clean up. I was cleaning up my house and blasting Monica on my surround sound while trying to enjoy a little moment of peace. I was at a place in life where I was putting myself first before anyone else. As I collected my thoughts, I heard my phone going off.

"Hello?" I answered it without even looking at the name on the phone.

"Hello?" I said with more attitude because they weren't saying anything.

"Hey, girl! My bad. I got caught up in the news. Matter of fact, turn to it. That's the reason I called," Kiah said.

I turned my surround system on low and flicked to the local news, WALB. Kathy Hill was reporting on a murder that had taken place. I turned it up a bit so I could listen to every detail. The picture of Samual Harris appeared on the screen. The news showed different pictures of his achievements all over the screen as well as pictures of him and his family. It was crazy how the media could make you look like such an angel. She mentioned that he had been shot, and there were no suspects at the moment. I turned off the TV because I had heard enough.

"Look, my cousin told me that detectives are all over this case because they have a witness that caught someone on video that morning. Mo, you got me worried over here."

My whole body filled with goosebumps.

"Bitch, don't be worrying or stressing. I got this. Whatever they saw, it wouldn't show much. I never revealed my face."

"Mo, you sure about that?" Kiah said in a concerned voice.

"Yeah, this is just the beginning, Kiah. There are a lot of selfish men out there," I said with a smirk.

There was no turning back now. I was going to make every man in America know that a woman's wrath was powerful.

"Ok, you know I'm behind you all the way," she assured me.

My heart dropped when Kiah switched the conversation and started talking about her and Aubrey getting married. I mean, I was happy for her ass. But at the same time, I honestly didn't think Kiah was ready for such a commitment. Instead of sounding like a hating ass bitch, I told her I was happy for her and quickly switched the topic toward Detective Rolle. When Kiah found out that Marcus and Detective Rolle was the same man, she couldn't help but laugh.

"Bitch, you done killed two niggas, and you have got a crush on a damn Detective."

"Wrong. I don't have a crush on him."

"Girl, don't even lie. I saw how y'all looked at each other when we first met at Ms. Bessie's. I wanted to smack your ass when you told him you were married. Girl, you better have you some fun and get your pussy ate out or fucked."

I hollered into the phone because Kiah was a damn fool.

"I ain't bothered by another nigga right about now."

Kiah sighed but didn't say anything. Instead, we got on another topic. I told her that I wanted her to see if she could find out more about the video. After she told me she would, my mind was back at ease. Before we disconnected, she told me she was going to come over to get her money when she got the chance. I had just got off the phone with Kiah when my phone vibrated. It was a text message from her. She was advising me to hit Marcus up and try to get to know him better so I could find out more information. I didn't even think about it like that and decided fucking around with Marcus was definitely going to have its benefits. I didn't hesitate to shoot Marcus a text message.

**Me:** *Hey! Mr. Marcus, just to let you know, I will take you up on your offer.*

I jumped on Instagram until Marcus responded to my text. I took a couple of selfies of my new hairstyle because I knew I was crushing them hoes out there. As soon as I posted one picture, the likes came back to back.

**Marcus:** *Hey. I'm glad to hear from you. How you doing?*

He texted me back with smiley faces. I shook my head. It felt like we were in high school again.

**Me:** *Same here, so what's your plans?*

**Marcus:** *I'ma hit you up later.. I'm kinda busy dealing with a homicide case. As soon as I'm done I will text you back.*

**Me:** *Ok don't have me waiting.*

When my phone sounded off, I knew that it was a voice message. I called the person "The Voice" because it seemed like the perfect name for the person who was messaging me and sending me information on who to murk. I opened up my messages and noticed that the voice sent me a profile. I scanned it. The next victim on the list was an author named Paul White.

"This will be the last chapter of your life once I'm done with you," I muttered to myself.

When my phone began to ring, I was shocked to see The Voice's name pop up on my phone.

"Hello."

"Congratulations on your last job. I'm offering you $40,000 for Paul White's head," the automated voice said.

I was just about to speak when the call was disconnected.

A Day Later

Finding Mr. Paul White's residence was a piece of cake. He lived in a beautiful two-story home in the Doublegate subdivision. The good thing about this one was that pine trees bordered his yard, so I could creep up without being spotted by nosey ass neighbors. Taking out my camera, I took a couple of pictures so I could study the house. Pulling off, I noticed that someone was watching me, so I politely waved at them. They rudely shut the curtain.

Before I took it in for the day, I had another mission I had to take care of. I pulled up to the Department of Motor Vehicles. It was hard as hell to find a parking spot because the place was swamped. When I stepped inside I saw three people standing in line waiting. The first woman was plus-sized with two kids that were kicking her ass. The second woman had to be a college student because she had an innocent look on her face. When I saw the third woman, I got a vibe, but I couldn't tell at the moment if it was good or bad. She was dark-skinned, slim, had her weaved pulled up in a ponytail, and wore very little makeup. Her swag was on point, and it looked like she had a little money.

"Excuse me."

She turned around, looking surprised.

"Not to be rude or anything, but are those Gucci sandals?" I asked and pointed at her feet.

"Yes, they are. They haven't hit the rack yet," she informed me.

"Nice."

She just smiled.

"I like your hair," she said.

"Thanks. My girl, Yaz, did it."

"I heard about her, but she stays packed. If you don't know somebody, you won't get in."

I told her I could get her in if she wanted me to.

"What's your name?" I asked.

"My name is Kim. What about yours?"

"My name is Monica, but people call me Mo."

I pulled my phone out and logged her number in. When it was her turn to log mine in, I noticed a certain picture on her home screen page. It kind of knocked me off balance because I was not expecting it.

"I will call you, girl, so we can make a hair appointment," Kim said while gathering her things. As she was about to walk off, I gently grabbed her.

"Aye, I was just thinking... uh... I noticed your husband on your phone. Would you like to come over for dinner?" I waited for her response.

I could see the hurt in her eyes. "Well, I would love that, but..." she paused for a minute. I thought she was about to fall on the floor. "He's not my husband. He's a guy I was dating."

Tears ran down her face. I gave her some tissue from an agent's desk and got the information I came for at the same time.

"He must have broken up with you," I asked, trying to get to the bottom of the story.

"No, he was murdered."

Her tears were nonstop. I extended my shoulder to her.

"It's going to be okay.

"How long were y'all dating?" I asked her.

"His name was Johntavious, and we dated five years."

My heart was filled with a powerful, violent rage. I knew he was cheating but not for that long.

"Y'all had kids together?"

I had to see if he had more kids out there.

"No. He was married, though," she said out of shame. She looked down at the floor.

"It's okay, I've messed with a married man before." I lied.

I didn't want to make her uncomfortable so lying was the best option.

"Have you ever seen his wife before?"

"No. The fact he was married, I refrained from

showing up at the funeral. The only thing I knew was that she was a lazy woman. That's all he used to tell me about her."

I shook my head. It's wild how men lie just to get what they want out of women. She told me more about their relationship. The more she told me, the more I plotted her death. I walked her to the car. The black bitch was driving a midnight blue Mercedes Benz E Class Coupe AMG with chrome rims. I knew Jihad had his hand in that. Wow! Men ain't shit. That's why my favorite book was *Trust No Man* by Cash. I should've paid more attention to things, and maybe shit wouldn't have gotten this far. *Where did I go wrong?* I kindly waved as she drove off. I started the engine up and jetted out of there because I had a million and one things on my mind.

# Chapter 14

## Monica

It was late at night and everyone was in bed. As for me, I was tucked behind the steering wheel in front of Paul White's house, ready to bring his whole world crashing down with my terror. I could see the glow from the TV, so I knew that he was downstairs. I opened the door to my left and proceeded to the side door. I felt like Cat Woman with my all black on. I picked the lock, and it popped right open. As I pushed the door, I heard footsteps coming from the inside toward my direction, so I dashed into some bushes next to the door. If he put his head out, I was going to shoot it off his shoulders. The light flicked off. Within seconds, it was dark again.

That was my cue to strike. The bushes must have had some thorns on it because my hands were bleeding a little. It didn't faze me at all, though. I stepped into the kitchen, and dishes filled the sink.

"Nasty motherfucker," I said to myself.

The TV was so loud that it was about to give me a headache. I saw his wide-bodied ass sitting on the couch, eating popcorn. It was so dark in the room that he didn't see me coming.

*CLACK!* The butt of the gun hit the side of his head.

"Shut the fuck up. If you move, I'll blast your head off."

"I… I… I…" he tried to speak.

*CLACK!* I hit him again.

"Shut the fuck up! Again, if you say another word, it better be worth losing your life."

I kept the gun pointed at him and flicked on the light switch. This fat, nasty motherfucker had food all over the floor. I threw the zip ties to his feet. At first, he hesitated, but the barrel was aimed at him, making him realize that it would be a dumb decision. I zip-tied his feet then both of his hands. I pulled out a syringe that I mixed with cocaine and another deadly poison.

"No, no… Please do—"

I cut him off with a slap in the face.

"Don't say a fucking word!"

The aggravation and frustration had me just wanting to unload the whole clip on him. I shot the drug into his system. Once it was in, his head fell back, and his eyes rolled to the back of his head. I knew then that it was over. I just had to top it off with a headshot. Once I pulled the trigger, his head busted like a watermelon. Then, I shot the TV to seal the deal. I exited the house and hit the road.

The more rage I released gave me a feeling of pleasure. I grabbed my phone and noticed I had some missed calls—two unknown callers, one from Marcus, and one from Kiah. Kiah left me a voice message singing a Faith Evans song. She put a smile on my face. Before she hung up, she said I'd been busy, and I'd been neglecting her. The next message was from Marcus. He stated that he wanted to take me to dinner. I couldn't help but smile. The way he was with words had my hormones on fleek. I had not been touched since Jihad and I had messed around. It would be nice if Marcus picked a fruit off the tree of life.

"Does he deserve it?" I asked out loud.

## Two Days Later

I flipped on the local news and saw that they had found Fat Ass. I could tell the news reporters and police were furious because of all the murders with no suspects. The streets would be loaded with cops very soon. I called Kiah and got no answer. Marcus was not picking up either. I headed to the kitchen to get me Rachel Ray on. I whipped up some pancakes, bacon, and cheese eggs.

*RING! RING!*

"Hey!" I greeted Kiah.

"Sup, bitch!" she shouted back.

"Just getting my cooking game on."

"Really, bitch? You know I love your cooking."

I was smacking in her ear, teasing her.

"Mmm, it's sooo good." I finished teasing her about my cooking.

A lot of people said I had a gift in the kitchen. I can make boiled water taste better than wine itself. Kiah suggested we hit Ms. Bessie's up later to discuss our other personal business issues. Once I ended the call, I saw that Marcus had sent me a text message.

**Marcus:** *Hey beautiful. Sorry about the other day. Can I make it up to you by taking you out?*

He always sent me smiley faces with his texts. Marcus was a handsome man with the potential to become my man one day. I just hated that he walked into my life at the wrong time. At the moment, it was hard for me to trust anyone with a dick.

**Me:** *I understand your job title, and yes I would love for that to happen.*

I sent him some smiley faces back. We had a moment

of sending funny pictures to each other to show our interest in one another. I let him know I would need to meet up with Kiah later. He told me he understood because he had to work late because of a new murder. If only he knew who was the real suspect was. I kept that thought to myself. After I was done texting, I jumped in the shower. After I hopped out the shower, I was in a "Ready to Take Over the World" mood. I put on my skin-tight Versace lace dress and opened my jewelry box to the Tiffany collection. The first thing that caught my eye was a double-strand necklace with diamonds that were to die for. As I wrapped the necklace around my small neck, I felt like the queen of Egypt.

"Damn, I look good."

As I posed in the mirror, I began to sing Mary J. Blige's song "Fine." After I was dressed, I texted Kiah to let her know I was on my way.

I hit the alarm to my Aston Martin Rapides and waved at my nosey neighbor. I hit the push to start button, and the engine came on with a thundering roar. I tilted my hater blockers down. I was on point from top to bottom. Glancing at the phone, I noticed that Kim had texted me and hoped that we could get together this week. I let her know that would be cool. Cruising through the city, there was an accident on Broad Street. A pickup truck ran into a beat-up Honda Accord. Good thing no one was hurt. I took a detour to Pine Street so I wouldn't get held up on my way to Ms. Bessie's.

The place was packed like always. Kiah texted me earlier to let me know she had already made it. I should've known that hungry lion was ready to eat. I was glad she already had our seats. The aroma from the steamed collard greens smelled so delicious.

"Mo, over here!" Kiah screamed across the room.

I strolled past all the other people in line. A lot of them had a sour look because they had to wait in that long ass line. Plus, everything I had on was worth more than their monthly paycheck. They better had kept all their comments to their fucking selves before they met the she-devil inside of me.

"Good to see you, Kiah," I said, giving her my famous hugs and kisses.

As we pulled back, I glanced at my girl. She was rocking Ferragamo from head to toe. The pants she wore showed off all the curves she had. My bitch was looking good.

"I like that," I complimented her.

"You know how I get down," she said then got up and

dropped it like it was hot.

That fool is something serious.

We got our plates and started choosing food from the buffet. I started with a small chicken salad with thousand island dressing. Kiah, on the other hand, had mashed potatoes and a huge prime rib steak. I just shook my head at her because that girl didn't play when it came down to food.

"What?" Kiah asked with a perplexed look.

"I'm just looking at all that food you about to intake," I answered.

She cut the steak and tried to feed it to me. She and I both laughed when I snatched my head away.

"What's really been going on with you? I've not seen you in like forever. All we do is text, but you ain't came and chilled with me in like forever." she said with a puppy dog look.

I threw a balled-up napkin in her direction.

"Just been handling some business. Guess what, girl!" I said and hit her hand to indicate that I had some juicy tea. Kiah's eyes opened wide.

"I saw Jihad's son at the funeral, and I met one of the females he was cheating on me with. Apparently, he'd been with her for five years."

Kiah put her hand on her mouth in total shock. I nodded my head in agreement. Kiah dropped her fork and smashed her fist against the table. The other guests started looking and talking amongst themselves. Kiah gave them a defiant look, and they focused their attention back to their plates. She came over and put her arm around my shoulder.

I let her know everything would be okay. I gave her the scoop and every detail on how it went down.

"Glad you offed that nigga," Kiah said.

"So, what's up with this wedding?" I asked, trying to get the focus off me.

"Well, we ain't made a solid date yet," she said.

"I'm so proud of you, girl." I gave her a huge hug.

After we ate and filled our bellies, the check came. I swiped the machine and left a nice tip for the young waiter. After I left the restaurant, I stopped by the mall to grab a couple of Gucci bags and some more Gucci shades. I was feeling like I had the world in the palm of my hands.

Once I made it home, it felt like the South Pole. The A/C was piping. I stripped down to nothing but my panties, wrapped up in my thick, soft blanket on the couch, and watched an episode of *Martin* until I fell asleep.

# Chapter 15

## Monica

I had to admit, I almost declined Marcus's offer at the last minute. Something inside of me told me to give him a chance. Today marks a new chapter of a new life. I strolled past the mirror a couple of times before I felt comfortable. Never give too much on the first date. My old-fashioned ways were still in tune with me, so I kept it very simple but still sexy as usual. I was sporting a nice Louis Vuitton cream-colored dress with some open-toe Louis Vuitton heels. I wanted to shine a little, so I put the Todd Red bracelet on my wrist. I sprayed Rihanna's fragrance all over my body.

*KNOCK! KNOCK!*

As I opened the door, his Fahrenheit cologne invaded my nostrils. It had triggered the switch to my hormones.

"Calm down," I had to tell my girl down there.

I was at the point where I wanted to kidnap someone and turn him into my personal sex slave. I never was a person that had to have it all time, but a woman does have her needs. You can be holy, but holy still had to catch a good nut.

"Hello, Mr. Rolle," I greeted, gesturing for him to come in.

Before he took a step forward, he had one hand behind him.

"This is for you, beautiful." He handed me a rose.

That was a brownie point on his behalf. It kind of let me know that he had been paying attention.

"Thank you! C'mon, have a seat."

I pointed to the area where I wanted him to sit until I was ready. I placed the rose in the flower vase. He looked like he'd stepped out of a G Magazine photoshoot. He was rocking a black Armani suit. He was a classic man and had on some Stacy Adams dress shoes.

"You have a nice condo," he said as he examined the African pieces on the wall.

"Thank you. I just had to change locations. Too many memories back home," I added.

I grabbed my purse and signaled to him that I was ready to go. As I was about to close the door, he placed a kiss on my lips.

"Don't think because you gave me a rose you deserve a kiss," I teased him, strolling past him and making my ass jiggle.

I looked back to see if he was enjoying the show. He

had a big smirk on his face. He hit the alarm on his whip. Marcus' ass was pushing a clean, classy, candy-red Mercedes Benz S class with black leather interior and candy apple red stitching. As I was about to reach for the handle, but Marcus said, "No, not yet," and pulled the door open for me.

He was such a gentleman. I couldn't help but think this night was going to turn out really great. Before he started the engine, he grabbed my hand. Suddenly, my panties got wet. This nigga had me feeling shit I ain't felt in a very long time.

"Thank you for allowing me to have this time with you," he said while licking his lips. He reminded me of LL Cool J. He was turning me on with everything he did. I just remained calm until I saw his deep dimples. That's when my system went into overdrive, and my pussy jumped repeatedly.

"You're welcome. A lot of men don't get this chance with me, so don't mess it up," I said with confidence.

"I gotcha, beautiful. You're in good hands."

He opened his hands up, and it reminded me of the Allstate logo. I just smiled at that fool. He started the engine up, and the whole dashboard lit up. The sound system was on point. R. Kelly's "I've Been Looking for

Love" was coming from the speakers.

"That's my jam!" I started singing to the music. That song took me back to the old days.

"I love me some R&B," he said.

"I hear ya," I shot back.

I glanced into his hazel eyes. We had eye sex for at least thirty seconds until my phone snapped me out of my trance.

"What, nosey?"

I knew it was Kiah's crazy ass about to ask me one thousand questions about him.

"Did I disturb something?" she asked.

"Maybe," I shot back, glancing at him because she was screaming into the phone.

"Just checking on you, making sure my bestie is ok."

"Aww, how sweet. I think Marcus will keep me safe."

When I mentioned his name, his whole facial expression changed. I winked at him. That just topped it off.

"Okay then. Just remember this…"

"What?"

"Use a condom." She burst out laughing.

"Bye, girl," I shot back real quick.

She knew how to keep a smile on my face. I didn't

know what I would do without her. Once I ended the call, he had all his pearly white teeth showing. I just hoped he knew what he was getting himself into dealing with me. I gave Marcus my full attention again.

"That must've been your sister?" he asked.

"You could say that. We've been around each other all of our lives."

"That's good to know. She seems like she brings the other side out of you."

"What side?"

"The side where you let your hair down."

"I don't show that side to a lot of people, to be honest. You're the first man I've been around besides my husband."

"Wow! How long have you been married?" he asked.

"For ten years."

"Yes, I remember you telling me that back when I was trying to holler at you. He was a lucky man."

"Too lucky," I said.

He was speechless. The car got silent. I clicked the stereo to repeat the song. I closed my eyes, sat back, and enjoyed the music. We pulled up to this restaurant called Jewel, one of the world-famous restaurants in the South. I'd been trying to go for a long time but never had the opportunity to come. The parking lot was not that packed, which I found odd.

"You're going to like this," he said with a smirk on his face.

I was not expecting him to be so nice, but I also knew the games men played to get you to fall for them.

We entered the double doors. I thought I was hallucinating when I read the banner in the middle of the floor that read *Monica, Thank You* in bold letters.

I couldn't believe this man had everything catered for me. Tears started flowing slowly down my cheeks. I was speechless. The host greeted us and walked us to our table. The table was decorated with various kinds of roses.

"Thank you for all of this," I said, giving a kiss on the cheek.

He just smiled and pulled out my chair. The waiter approached the table.

"Mr. Marcus, may I take your order?"

He paused for a second and looked at me with his sexy ass. He had me about to squirt in my seat. I had to keep a handle on myself.

"You ready to place your order?" he asked me.

He caught me off guard because I was in a very deep

trance, thinking about his dimples.

"Give me a minute. I need to go to the ladies' room," I responded, and the young waiter said he would be back.

I got up, but before I could walk away, I heard, "Aye, don't jet out on me."

He had a smirk on his face. I looked back and blew him a kiss. He caught it and put it on his lips.

I had to get away because I had to get him out of my system. I had to take control of the situation. Things were getting too heated. He was a charming guy, and I didn't want things to move too fast. I looked in the mirror.

"C'mon, Monica, behave yourself," I said to myself.

It was so hard to stay focused when I hadn't felt like this in a long time. I got myself together and headed back to the table. He didn't allow me to sit without him pulling my chair out for me.

"You're such a gentleman," I told him.

"My mother told me to treat a woman like she's worth the world," he said.

"So, what do you think is my worth?" I questioned his statement.

"You're a special woman."

I took a sip of wine from my glass. Before I could take another sip, he grabbed my hand and looked into my eyes.

"You got the three S's."

I gave him a look of intrigue.

"Monica, you are smart, sophisticated and very sexy," he said and then licked his damn lips. He had to be stopped because he was too much for me. The waiter brought our meals.

"I took the initiative in placing our orders." Marcus winked at me.

He ordered us a big bottle of Domaine Jean-Louis Chave red wine, filet mignon, top sirloins, pork chops, Omaha steak burgers, baked potatoes, and caramel apple tarts. The aroma of it had me ready to devour it like a lion seeking his prey.

"I've really been enjoying myself. Thanks."

The food was totally delicious. I would definitely be coming back.

"No need to thank me. I thank you for allowing me to spend time with a beautiful queen such as yourself." He had me blushing.

"So, tell me about yourself," I suggested.

"Well, let me start by saying I have been single for six years because I was supposed to have gotten married, but that didn't turn out."

I cut in, "What happened?"

"On our wedding day, she left me a note saying she was not in love with me anymore."

I grabbed my mouth in total shock.

"I couldn't imagine going through something like that. My life has been a living hell, but the one day that is supposed to be the happiest day of a person's life was the worst experience ever."

"I'm sorry to hear about that," I said in a concerned voice.

"No need to be because that taught me to just wait on God to send me my angel," he said while looking into my eyes. I felt goosebumps running up my thighs that had my treasure box throbbing.

We sat there for a while and chatted about his past. I told him how Jihad and I met and what I went through in our marriage. He couldn't believe that I was a victim. I told him I was a firm believer in God, but now, I had a lot on my plate. After talking and eating that wonderful meal, Marcus paid, and we headed back to my place.

"I really enjoyed myself tonight," I said, reaching into my purse for my keys.

"I hope this won't be the last time because you are a remarkable woman."

I felt his dick on my ass and the shit felt really good.

"Trust me it won't, cau—"

He cut me off with a kiss. He had his tongue in my mouth, and his lips were so soft. We kissed so passionately that it seemed like I was hearing fireworks. Thc way he caressed my breasts had my panties wet, and my body ached for him. I was up against the door kissing a man I barely even knew.

"I'm not ready yet," I confessed.

"I want you so bad, Monica. You just don't understand."

"Marcus, don't get it twisted. You're a great man, and I would love to take it there with you, but I'm not ready to be with another man yet."

I finally opened the door. The cool breeze hit my body. He was still right on my heels.

"I understand you've been through a lot, but everyone ain't the same, Monica. I want to treat you like the queen you are."

Marcus was a good man, but he came into my life at the wrong time.

"I feel what you're saying, but Jihad damaged my heart. It's hard for me to trust anybody again."

We were standing so close that his dick felt so good. I

put my hands on his chest to put some space between us. Things were getting heated.

"Monica, it's time to move on. You got to let him go. Until then, I'm gonna be here waiting on that day," he said, giving me a very sensual look as he licked his sexy ass lips.

"Why?" I questioned his loyalty.

"'Cause a woman like you don't come around every day."

"What happens if I never do?"

"Well, we have to wait and see."

He kissed me on my forehead then walked backward until he made it to his car. Before he got in, he pointed at his watch. I just grinned and closed the door behind me.

"What am I going to do?" I said to myself.

I headed upstairs to fill the tub with warm water so I could soak my body and sip on some wine. Sometimes, situations can change you. I was feeling good, and I was really happy. I laid in the bed listening to Mary J. Blige's *My Life 2* CD until I fell asleep.

# Chapter 16

## Monica

"Hey, I got a client. I'm sending the information," The Voice said.

The text message came immediately. When I saw who it was, I couldn't believe it, but I had to handle my business. I put it to the back of my mind and decided to hit my best friend up. I dialed her phone, and she picked up on the third ring.

"Heyyyyyy!" Kiah screamed excitedly.

"How is everything with you?"

"I should be asking you that." She giggled.

While I was talking to her, Marcus was texting me. Ever since that day, he made sure I got a "good morning" message.

"You still there?" She punched a number.

"Yeah, my bad. I was sending Marcus a text."

"This man got you messed up, Mo."

She burst out laughing and started singing "It's Love in the Air."

"It's not like that. He cool, but I can't go down that road again."

I had to get that out of her mind.

"Why? He's not ugly. You gotta let go 'cause you're a good person, Monica."

Whenever she called me by my first name, she was as serious as a heart attack. I took her words in, but I had a mission to complete before I'd be ready to start a relationship again. Marcus sent me a picture of him standing next to an empty lot. The text read: *Our family will start here.* Wow, this man was something serious.

"Why you doing this to me?" I said out loud.

"What did I do?" Kiah asked in confusion.

I had so much going on that I forgot she was on the phone.

"Sorry, Kiah. I was thinking out loud."

When Kiah started asking about my date, I couldn't help but beam. I told her how wonderful the date went. I even told her that I was falling for him, but I wasn't ready yet. She told me to pray about things. She was not the praying type, so I gave it consideration before I turned it down. Kiah and I talked for over an hour before we disconnected the call.

Later That Day

I pulled out my iPhone and logged into my Facebook account. I noticed I had several messages. I checked them and didn't respond because most of them were ugly guys trying to holla at me, and I wouldn't give them the time of day. I saw that Kim had sent me a text message which got my attention.

**Kim:** *Hey Monica, just checking on you. I hope everything is okay. We need to get up together... smiley faces.*

**Me:** *I've been okay, just been handling things. We can get together this weekend if things play out great.*

She and I had been texting ever since the day at the DMV. She seemed down to earth, but I hated that she got caught in the middle. Everybody was going to pay big for breaking my heart. I meant that. I had been waiting in my car for two whole hours for my next victim to arrive. I was hot and exhausted. I was just about to dip out and come back later on when a sky-blue Chevy Tahoe pulled up. I saw that he was not alone as the passenger door open and a woman stepped out. She was a dark-skinned, slim chick. I did not recognize who she was due to the distance from where I was parked. The two of them kissed each other like they were in their bedroom.

*It's so crazy how a person can stand in front of the congregation and preach about the Lord's work, but be living in the Devil's world,* I said to myself.

I waited another thirty minutes before I crept up to the front door and twisted the knob. It was locked.

*Check the mat,* my inner voice rang in my head.

When I pulled out the key, I just shook my head.

*Why are people so predictable?* I thought.

I slowly opened the door. The smell of evil was in the atmosphere.

"Yes, daddy, give it to me!" the woman moaned out.

I heard her voice coming from the open bedroom door on the right. Before I entered the room, I searched the house to make sure no one else was in the home. When I entered the room, my face went into total shock, not by the performance, but because of who it was. It was Jihad's cousin KeKe. That tramp was fucking the preacher. *It must run in the family.* I stood there for a brief second to get my head together.

*BOOM!* The television came crashing down. Glass flew everywhere. They nearly jumped through the wall. Both of them had sweat running from their bodies. Just that fast, it turned from a sex scene to a Monica takeover. I pulled out my .9mm pistol with the silencer and pointed at them.

"Well, well, well, what do we have here?" I said with

a smirk on my face, even though the ski mask hid it.

"Please don't kill me!" she begged, wrapping the sheets around her body.

"I'm not gonna kill you..." I paused for a second and turned my attention to him. "But I am going to kill him."

I hit him across the temple.

*WHAM!* He fell to the center of the bed holding his head.

"You're supposed to be a damn preacher!" I yelled out emotionally.

I took my mask off. KeKe looked at me like I was Lucifer himself.

"Monica, what are you doing?" he pleaded for his life.

"Doing my duty. I'm putting people like you to waste."

I put the pistol to his forehead. My whole hand was shaking.

"Stop all that crying, bitch, before I blast the tears off yo' fuckin' face, hoe!"

I was so frustrated. Looking at her reminded me of him.

*WHAM! WHAM!*

I hit KeKe directly in her face, causing blood to fly

out of her mouth.

"Mmm, please…" KeKe begged for mercy.

My assault continued. I kicked her dead in the face. The kick laid her out on the floor. With all of that going on, the good ole preacher tried to creep out of the room. I gave him a shot of hot lead to his ass.

*POW! POW!*

He flew forward through the threshold. I walked over to where he was at and flipped him on his back.

"The Lord is my shepherd…" I cut him off and put my foot on his throat because I didn't want to hear that shit.

"Don't start praying now, bitch!" I kneeled down.

"I'm about to send your ass straight to hell."

I pointed the gun at his head. He closed his eyes, ready to endure the impact. Right before I was about to pull the trigger, that bitch KeKe rushed me from behind. The gun went off but missed him. She jumped on top of me and threw a book, but no connection was made. I somehow flipped her over with all the strength I had inside of me. I swung really quick and punched blood from that bitch's mouth. I gave her two more combo punches.

"Take that, pussy ass hoe."

I was giving it to her with all I had. She still had some buck in her. She charged at me, and I gave her a roundhouse kick, sending her to the wall nightstand. I grabbed the gun and shot that bitch in the head. I gave the hoe something to think about too. Then, I walked over to that lying ass motherfucker and emptied the whole fucking clip on his ass.

I was so glad it was all over with. I grabbed my ski mask and ran out the door. The streets were still moving slowly just like I liked it. I dashed to my vehicle and sped off. I sent a text message to The Voice to let them know I was done. Within minutes, an alert popped up on my phone, letting me know I had a new deposit that had posted for $30,000. I just smiled.

"Payback's a real bitch," I mumbled.

I pulled up to my condo. I noticed a small note on my door. When I read it, I smiled because Marcus was still thinking of me.

*I NEED YOU! I LOVE YOU! I MISS YOU!*

He was so charming, but that's how all niggas acted it in the beginning. I was not trying to go through that again. All I wanted to do was get in the tub, soak, and fall asleep to my girl Tamia.

# Chapter 17

## Marcus

The office was busy like always. Different officers were trying to solve their cases. For me, all I could think about was Monica.

*KNOCK! KNOCK!*

A knock on my office's door took me out of my trance immediately.

“Come on in,” I demanded.

I really didn’t feel like being fucked with today. My partner came through the door with a serious look on her face, so in my line of work, I knew there had been another homicide.

“What’s going on, Ms. McDonald?” I asked, trying to read her mind.

“Well, we got two pieces this morning. They were just discovered an hour ago,” she said while taking a seat.

“Gender?” I asked.

She paused for a second, trying to search through the paperwork.

“Male and female.”

I gathered my things and signaled to her that we were

about to hit the streets. We got in the unmarked car. When we were pulling out, my phone started ringing. I answered it on the second ring.

"Hello."

"Good morning, handsome. How are you?" Monica asked.

She sounded so good in the morning. She had a nigga wanting to make love to her voice.

"What have you done today?"

"Just keep you on my mind, but can I get at you later? I'm about to go check this homicide."

"Okay, I'm not going to hold you up. Just call me later."

"Will you do something for me?"

"What?" she said in confusion.

"Stay beautiful

"Aw, you're so sweet."

I could tell I had her blushing. The thought of her blushing had me thinking about kissing her lips again. We said our goodbyes. I looked at my partner, and she had a crazy look on her face.

"What's wrong with you?" I asked.

"Question is… What's wrong with you, Mr. Lover Man?" She burst out laughing.

"This woman I'm dating is so incredible," I confessed.

I wasn't the type of person to talk about my relationships at work, but since we'd been partners for a while, I felt like I could trust her.

"Do you remember that woman whose husband was found dead in Texas?"

"Yeah, what about her?" she asked.

"Well, I kind of date her." She put her hands on her face in shame.

"I can't believe you," she responded.

I was lost. I had no clue why it was such an issue.

"What you mean?"

I pulled the car behind the rest of the unmarked cars that were already at the scene.

"You're wrong, Marcus." Right before I was about to speak, she cut me off. "I thought you had more respect for yourself. That woman lost her husband, and you know she's at her lowest stage in life right now. You saw how beautiful she was, and you had to proceed with it. It's just like a man to always prey on a woman's weakness."

She opened the door and slammed it before I could plead my case. Was she right? Was I wrong? I didn't know what to think. I stayed in the car for a hot minute so

I could think about what she had just told me. The tapping on my window brought me back to reality.

"May I help you?" I asked her.

"Yes, my name is Tammie Young. I am the crime scene investigator. Your partner sent me this way. I'm supposed to inform you about what's going on," she said.

She had a light caramel complexion and stood at five feet eleven with a nice little curvy shape. She was an attractive female, but she wasn't my type. I only had my eyes for one woman.

"I hope everything's good."

"Of course. Word around the department is you have the biggest percentage of solved cases."

"Yeah, I'm blessed for that," I boasted and beat on my chest. We both burst out laughing.

"Lately, these killers have been swift. They leave no evidence," I said.

"No worries, killers always leave some type of evidence behind."

We headed into the house. It was marked off with crime scene tape. The house had a foul odor to it. I grabbed a small face mask because I couldn't stomach the smell this time. I saw that it must have been a violent fight. I could tell it wasn't a robbery because nothing was out of place. I grabbed a camera and took a couple of pictures, trying to piece together what went wrong. I saw an older man lying on his back with multiple gunshot wounds to his body.

*He must've made someone mad,* I thought to myself.

The female lay there with a gunshot wound between her eyes. She had to see that coming.

*Oh my God... I'm so wrong,* I said to myself. Blood was everywhere from the walls to the floor to the ceiling. It was a terrible and violent sight.

"Detective Rolle, come here," Tammie commanded.

She handed me a small earring. I examined it closely and tucked it into a small bag from my pocket. *This cannot be possible.* I kept to myself for a minute and didn't say anything to anyone. Tammie continued to gather all the evidence, and I signaled to my partner to come over to where I was standing.

"Yes, Marcus?" she answered.

"I'm about to let them wrap up. I gotta head somewhere."

She was puzzled and did not understand my disposition.

"What's up? Tell me," she insisted, but I had to handle things by myself.

“I gotta do this alone. I’m gonna get at you later.”

I dashed off and headed to my car and got inside. I smashed my hand on the steering wheel.

“This can’t be happening. God, let me be wrong about this.” I started the car and got ghost.

# Chapter 18

## Zykiah

"Shit! Give it to me!" I yelled as Aubrey sucked my pussy. He had the best head game I'd ever had.

"How it feel, baby?" he asked, digging deep in with his tongue.

I could feel all of him in my stomach. Damn, where had this man been all my life? He gripped my ass cheeks. It felt so good. He grabbed me and flipped me on my stomach. I was disabled. He slapped the hell out of my thigh. That shit turned me on more. I put my ass in the air and my finger in my mouth. I licked it and then used it to play in my pussy. When I took it out, I put two in my mouth.

"Yum!" I tasted delicious. My cream was all over my fingers. He inserted his dick inside me, and I jumped.

"Bounce that pussy on this dick."

He slapped my ass, and I threw it back harder.

"Just like that!" Aubrey groaned as he stuck his thumb in my ass.

"Oh shit, daddy, I'm about to cum!"

"Cum on this dick," he commanded.

He started stroking at a faster pace then pulled my hair just how I liked it. Cum started running all over his dick. I was soaking wet. I could hear the wetness of my pussy as his dick slammed into me.

"Yesss, daddy!" I moaned out.

He was ripping my insides up. He grabbed both of my shoulders and started driving his giant, black dick in my ass. The pain shot through my body. It allowed me to bust back to back. The shit was so marvelous. I felt the sweat dripping off his body. The headboard was knocking all the pictures off the wall. I put my hand up to signal him to slow down. He just slapped it away.

"I ain't about to stop. You better take this dick."

I cried out as I started biting the bed sheets.

"Who pussy this is?"

"Yours, daddy," I mumbled.

"I can't hear you."

"Yours, daddy!" I screamed louder.

When he busted his nut, I thought it was over, but he wasn't through with me just yet. Instead, he laid down on his back and pulled me on top of him. I straddled him and started rotating my hips in a circular motion.

"Mmmm," he moaned with his eyes closed.

The more he moaned, the faster I started popping my

pussy. I used my two fingers to massage my clit as his eyes rolled to the back of his head.

"I'm about to cum all over this dick."

I pressed my nails into his chest. My sweet cream fell out of me like a waterfall.

"Yes, daddy, mmm."

I bit my bottom lip with my eyes closed, enjoying the pleasure. My big daddy was showing out.

"Babe, I'm cumming."

He released every ounce of his life inside of me. I immediately fell on his chest, breathing hard as hell. It seemed like every time we fucked, it was greater than the last time.

"Baby, I love you so much that words cannot describe," I confessed to my future husband.

"Boo, I love you too. You make a nigga feel loved. I'm glad we found each other."

"Babe, I want me and you to go on vacation with Monica and Marcus. What you think about that?"

"Baby, I will love that. Just come up with a date, baby girl."

We held each other until we fell asleep in each other's arms. I put all the niggas I was fucking around with on the block list. Aubrey was the only man I wanted to spend the rest of my life with. I didn't have time to be playing games any longer.

# Chapter 19

## Monica

It was a bright and beautiful Saturday afternoon. Kim and I had just seen the new *Straight Out of Compton* movie. I really enjoyed Kim's company, but I wished Kiah could've been with us. After the movie ended, we headed to get some lunch. Jimmy's Hot Shack was packed, so I decided to go through the drive-thru instead.

"What's your plan for the summer?" Kim asked while chowing down on some hot dogs from Jimmy's.

"Well, me and my girlfriend are going on a little vacation. It's kinda like a double date thing."

As we talked, I rolled down the window to get the onion smell out. Jimmy's had some good hot dogs, but the hot dogs' odor was always strong.

"That should be nice. I wish me and… never mind."

I could tell she wanted to say more, and I was curious to know what she was thinking.

"Go ahead. Spill the tea," I insisted.

I muted the music because I wanted to hear every detail.

"Well, my husband, Aubrey, is cheating on me," she

slowly said before putting her head down in shame.

It was no way that Aubrey could be the same nigga that Kiah was fucking with. No, it couldn't be. Instead of jumping to conclusions, I decided to listen as she went more into detail.

"Aww, sorry to hear that. How do you know?" I questioned.

"Yeah, I know he is because I followed him to her house. I was about to get out, but my pride didn't allow me to."

*Would her pride not allow her to?* I just laughed to myself. *Now, you got pride?* I didn't say anything; I just listened to her confess.

"I waited until they went inside and left a small note on her windshield."

When she said those five words, my heart sunk into my lap. I knew she could only be talking about one person. *Could that be possible? How do I tell her?*

"Wow, that's crazy! Men are something serious. All men are natural dogs," I added.

To be honest, I didn't give a damn about what she was going through. My inner-self was telling me to jump across the seat and beat the living shit out of her ass. Nevertheless, I had something planned very special for her ass. As she wiped the tears from her eyes, I reached over to try to cheer her up.

"Things are going to be okay. Just hold on," I lied.

We sat in the car for a couple of minutes chatting about her situation. I told her men didn't appreciate good women. She agreed and told me good women like herself didn't deserve to be mistreated. I didn't do too much commenting on what she was saying because she was a hypocrite. She wanted me to believe that she was a faithful woman. Sometimes, you had to let a person dig a bigger hole for themselves. When we pulled up at my place, Kim and I hopped out.

"Kim, I enjoyed your company today."

I gave her a small hug and watched her hop into her Infiniti QX70 truck. She didn't know what was coming her way. I entered my beautiful condo and jumped into the shower to clean up my body. When I got out, I lay across the bed and started thinking about Marcus. Next thing I knew, I grabbed my dildo out of my drawer and started to show love to my wet pussy. I dug in and out, causing my pussy to get wetter by each caress.

"Yesss," I moaned softly.

Pleasing myself felt so good. I busted my legs wide open so I could feel the inches of my dildo filling me up.

"Ohh!" I tilted my head back and rubbed my thumb over my clit.

"Shit!" I flipped over and arched my back, shaking my ass on the dildo.

"Marcus!" I couldn't believe I just called his name out. Suddenly, my phone started ringing. I tried to ignore the person's call, but they kept calling me.

"Yeah?" I answered irritably. They were calling at the wrong time.

"Did I call at the wrong time?" the man asked.

Whoever it was, I didn't recognize his voice because my mind was in another place. Once I came back to reality, I looked down at the screen. It was him of all people.

"Marcus, I'm sorry. I'm just horny as hell."

What I was thinking had slipped out, and I was in utter shock. I could tell I caught him off guard by the silence.

"You there? Because I was kind of in the middle of something."

"What were you in the middle of doing?" Marcus asked curiously.

"I was trying to please myself."

"Why are you doing that? I can beat that pussy down

a little bit," he boasted.

"I don't know. You may not keep up with this."

"I'm on my way," he said. Before I could say another word, the phone clicked in my face.

*No, he didn't.*

He must've flown over here because a few minutes later, I could hear his car outside. I went into the living room and opened the door before he could knock. When he saw me, our lips connected like magnets. His pink lips electrified the moistness between my thighs. I could feel the wetness dripping down my thighs. The towel that I had wrapped around my body fell to the floor. The front door never closed, so I was giving my neighbors a good show. While his tongue wrestled in my mouth, he palmed my soft ass. I didn't waste any more time. I pulled him all the way in and closed the door behind me. *I'm not freaky like that,* I thought. He pulled his shirt over his head, and I gladly got on my knees and unfastened his belt to take off his pants.

"Damn, your dick perfect," I mumbled while licking the tip of his dick.

I wet his dick up with my juicy mouth. I tried to do a magic trick and make the whole thing disappear. Due to his size, he had me gagging for air. While I was pleasing him, I shoved my hand into my pussy. I was horny as hell. I hadn't had an orgasm in four months. I needed it bad, and Marcus was giving me what I needed.

"Shit. This feels so good, baby," he cried out.

I could tell his nut was about to come. He increased his speed as I spread my legs. I started to jack his dick and spit on the tip.

"Aww, yes!" His hot nut shot on my breasts. I'll be damned if this nigga got the opportunity to say I swallowed him. He pulled me from the floor and carried me to the bedroom. We kissed passionately. The way he kissed me would make any bitch fall head over heels for him. I laid down on my back, and he immediately spread my thighs. His lizard tongue entered my core. It felt like heaven in my bedroom. I tried to run, but with the ninja grip he had on my thighs, I couldn't go anywhere.

"Daddy, eat this pussy!" I moaned out.

*SLURP! SLURP!* His tongue slurped up my juices. He fucked my pussy with his tongue as I gripped his head. He was taking me to another world and back again. He had the most beautiful eyes you could imagine. I could not take any more as he looked up at me while serving me up.

"I'm cumming! I'm cumming!" I screamed out

seductively.

"Shoot it all on my face," he encouraged me. I was creaming like a running fountain. I leaned back and patted my pussy to let him know I was ready for takeoff. I had my legs as wide as possible. He placed his massive dick inside of me, and I couldn't do anything but moan in pleasure.

"Sssss," I moaned slowly.

"I got you, beautiful," he said slowly in my ear.

I believed him, so I gave him my full body to control. He started off at a slow pace, moving back and forth.

"Ooh, that feels so good, Marcus."

I sucked his neck, and our bodies were in sync with each other. He hit every spot of my walls. The sensations he gave my body had me reaching the highest climax. It was the greatest moment ever.

"I'm cumming, daddy!"

"Cum on this dick!"

"Ohh, I'm cumming on that dick, daddy!"

We both released at the same time. I'd never felt like that before. I came five times in one night. My whole body was drained. I couldn't move anymore. I laid in his arms until I fell asleep.

# Chapter 20

## Marcus

It was early Saturday morning when I opened my eyes and saw Monica laid up next to me. Monica was the perfect definition of a woman in the streets and a freak in the sheets. She was a beautiful goddess that walked God's earth. I was intrigued. A woman that smart and loyal would be cherished by any man. I decided to surprise her by making breakfast because I knew she was all worn out from last night. I headed to the kitchen, opened the refrigerator, and grabbed some eggs, milk, butter, and other things that would delight us.

When I was all done, I crept back into the room. She was still knocked out like a baby. I was just about to wake her when I heard a phone go off. I wasn't the type to invade anyone's personal space, but my curiosity was killing me. So, I picked it up and noticed a text message that came through. I didn't open it. I read the first couple of titles. One read in bold letters, *I HAVE ANOTHER ONE.* I didn't know what she was into, but she had me pondering what "another one" meant. I just kept that in the back of my mind and hopped in the shower. I saw that she had some brand-new toothbrushes for guests, so I used one after I freshened up. Once I returned to the room, I could see that she was awake.

"Good morning, Sleeping Beauty!" I greeted her with a wink. Her hair was everywhere, but no matter what, she was still a sight for sore eyes.

"Good morning, Marcus." Her sweet voice lit my soul up.

She brushed her hair into place.

"I made you some breakfast. It's in the kitchen in the warmer."

Her eyes sparkled as she walked over to me and placed a soft kiss on my lips before heading in the kitchen to get her plate. When she took her first bite of pancakes and eggs, I watched as she closed her eyes like she was in heaven.

"Thank you for the breakfast. It's so good."

After she was done eating, I sat down on the bed with her and stared into her eyes. I cleared my throat before expressing my feelings toward her.

"I just want you to know… I cherish every moment in your presence." She blushed. "I'm dead ass serious."

Our faces connected, and our tongues entered each other's mouths, entangling in one of the greatest French kisses ever. My hands started making their way to her thighs, and my finger dipped into her honey box. She moaned slowly while sucking on my ear. I slid her on top of me before I slid inside of her.

"Yes, Marcus!" she yelled out as she bounced up and down on my manhood.

I was loving every second of her. I slapped her ass, gripped her hips, and then increased my speed. The sound of her moans was music to my ears and turned me on even more.

"Give it to me, baby," I encouraged as the pleasure continued.

I was about to flip her over when she suggested that she put in the work, so I lay back and let her work her magic.

"Oooh!" I moaned out with my eyes closed.

She was taking me on a rollercoaster ride by the way she was rotating her hips. *Shawty is bad as fuck.* That's all ran that through my head. She was putting something on the kid. The way her hands palmed my chest with her head tilted back was a great sight to watch. I could tell she was reaching her peak by the acceleration of her body. Her body began to shake. I knew she had reached her climax, and I soon followed her.

"Wow, you're going to make me miss work!" I teased her while trying to sneak another kiss in.

Monica got up and started to put on her bra and panties. Then, she sat on the bed and her whole demeanor changed.

"We need to talk," she said, looking me in my eyes.

I felt really awkward. The mood in the room switched from sexual to informal within a blink of an eye.

"About what, beautiful?"

I grabbed her hand, and she slightly jerked back. She had lost me because a few minutes ago, we were connecting like two love bugs.

"You're a good guy. Last night was incredible, and just a few minutes ago was amazing, but—"

I immediately cut her off.

"I understand all that. I understand you're scared, but I'm here," I defended myself.

I was discombobulated about her actions toward me.

"I can't do this. I don't want to mislead you," she proclaimed.

She hopped off the bed and headed toward the door. I ran after her and grabbed her by the arm. She pushed me off.

"Get your motherfucking hands off of me," she

demanded.

The expression on her face showed me that she had become another person that I didn't know.

"Marcus, it's time for you to go."

"Monica, I apologize for grabbing your arm, but don't treat me like I'm a stranger," I pleaded my case.

I was not trying to leave like this. She got silent and folded her arms. I started fixing my clothes and proceeded on my way out the door. Before I left her, I turned around and gave her a look of forgiveness.

"Mo, you got to let it go. Your past is hurting your future. When you're ready, I will be here," I said while trying to give her a kiss on the forehead, but she turned her head.

I left with an unbalanced state of mind. When I got in the car, my heart and mind were spinning. I glanced at my phone and noticed I had six missed calls. All of them were from my partner. *I wonder what she wants.* I was about to call her back, but I received a text from Monica.

**Monica:** *Marcus, you a great man, but right now my life is very difficult for you to understand. I'm sorry, but I just need time to think. I been through a lot and I don't want to go back down that road again. I hope you understand.*

**Me:** *Mo, I never met a woman like you before. I understand how you feel. I was in the same place you're sitting in now after my fiancé betrayed me. I took it out on everybody, but I realized she moved on with her life. That's when I let it go and let God deal with it, and that's when you appeared. Let it go. I'm here for you. :)*

I started the engine and proceeded on to my destination. I headed to the bar and got a couple of drinks to get my mind off of Monica. I drank until I couldn't feel my face.

# Chapter 21

## Zykiah

I had been working hard these past few days and was trying to get my body right for the trip that we were going to take. I wanted my body to look flawless in my two piece.

"Damn, bitch, you look good," I said to myself.

I scrolled through my Facebook and posted some pictures of my sculpted figure. *I should've been a model for a magazine or designer,* I thought. I flipped on my surround sound and played my light-skinned babe, J Cole. I twisted up a big blunt of Mary Jane and laid back.

*RING! RING!*

The phone took me out of my trance. I would've cursed the caller out, but I recognized it was my bitch calling.

"Heyyy, bitch!" I greeted my best friend.

"Hey, Kiah, how are you, girl?" she asked.

"Bitch, I'm doing good. I just rolled me a fat ass blunt and jamming to J. Cole while I think about my future with Aubrey. I can't wait until I walk down that aisle."

"Ugh."

That's all Mo said, so I knew something was wrong.

"What's wrong with you?" I questioned her, trying to get insight on what was on her mind.

"I'm just saying… Are you ready?"

"What you mean *'Am I ready?'*" I said with emphasis.

"Meaning, are you sure you ready to marry this man? Are you sure you know him like that? Everyone has secrets."

Her comment had me kind of upset and had me wondering could it be true about him.

"Sometimes, you let the past be in the past. If he does have a secret, I'm sure we can work it out because I have much love for his ass. Words can't explain it."

"What if he got a secret that can't be forgiven?"

That question took me off track. I had to come back real fast.

"Monica, listen to you. You done changed completely."

She tried to cut in, but I instantly snapped.

"You used to stay telling me about forgiveness. I used to try to get you to leave that asshole you were married to, but you stayed telling me about how God would bless you if you forgave him. I never understood that until I told Aubrey about my past life. He didn't look at me any differently. So, if I find out something, I'm pretty sure we can deal with it. Mo, baby, you have to let it go."

The phone got silent, and I took that opportunity to fill my wine glass up with a little Remy.

"Kiah, you know I want the best for you. That's all."

"Mo, I know you do, baby girl."

I quickly decided it was best to get off the topic of me getting married. Instead, I switched to be about her and her love life. I suggested that she give Marcus a chance at making her happy. She somehow still refused the advice I was giving. I just wished Mo would get out of the lifestyle she was living. If something happened to her, my life would be in a million pieces. I cleared my head of the unbearable thought.

Later That Day

I glanced in the mirror, making sure I was on point. I was rocking my cocaine white Coach sundress, matching baby doll Coach shoes, and my Coach clutch. I had just left Yaz's after getting my hair done again and was rocking a twenty-four-inch pineapple wave, lace front

Malaysian wig that she hooked up. I knew I looked like a top-notch bitch. I was known to slay hoes anyway. They knew I stayed on fleek. I grabbed my Coach clutch and headed out the door. The breeze was just right. It was the middle of June, so the weather was crazy down South. Some days, it will be hella hot, and then it could be as cold as ice on other days. I glanced at my windshield, and I noticed a small note.

"Oh, shit! I got a little secret admirer."

I read the note, and the words on the paper let me know it was a different type of letter. It read in bold letters:

*HEY HOMEWRECKER,*

*YOUR TIME IS COMING, TRUST ME*

"What the fuck!" I yelled out in frustration.

I started to scan the area, trying to see if anything was out of the ordinary. I was confused. Many questions came to my mind—*Who did this? Is my past relationship coming back to haunt me?* I had ruined a lot of marriages after Dewayne. I was puzzled. I had no clue, but I knew one thing… I had to hunt down my mystery woman before she took me out.

I sat in the driver's seat for a moment to gather my thoughts. Then, Mo's statement reminded me about

Aubrey.

"Is he the reason behind this?" I asked myself because I had to get to the bottom of this.

I pushed the start button to crank my whip. I put it in drive and headed on my new journey of getting to the bottom of this bullshit.

2 Days Later

My body was in so much pain, and my vision was also blurred. I heard a repeated beeping noise ringing in my ear. Once I gained consciousness, I realized I was in a hospital bed. I didn't know what happened or how I had even gotten there. I quickly paged a nurse so she could tell me what the fuck was I doing laid up in the hospital. Within seconds, a young woman came rushing over.

"She's opened her eyes."

That's all she kept saying with excitement written all over her face. *How long was I out?* I asked myself. I was in a private room. It was surrounded by balloons, teddy bears, and different bouquets of flowers. A few other nurses rushed into the room.

"Check her vital signs," the doctor commanded the nurses. They unbelted my arms.

"I… I…" I muttered something, but it was hard as hell to talk. My mouth was as dry as sandpaper.

"Keep your energy, Ms. Harris," the doctor ordered. All I saw were different nurses coming and going while writing on their pads. The first nurse I saw injected something into my arm.

"I… I…" I tried to speak again before I passed out.

## One Hour Later

"Wake up for me, Kiah."

When I opened my eyes, my beautiful sister was leaning over me.

"Lord, thank you!" Monica thanked God.

I tried to say something, but my voice wouldn't allow it. I motioned for the cup. She held it to my mouth. The juice was ice cold. It quenched my thirst.

"Mo… Mo!" I pushed out.

"Kiah, I'm here for you, baby."

She held one hand then kissed me on the forehead. I could tell she had been crying by the strain in her voice. My main concern was who put me here.

The young nurse came back to give me a liquid medication. It tasted awful. I wanted to spit that shit directly in her face, but she had been nothing but sweet to me. I didn't have the energy to do anything. The nurse left the room and informed me that she'd be back later to check in on me. My entire body was in so much pain, and my head was spinning nonstop. I was ready to get out of this room and back to my normal life.

"What happened to me?" I asked Monica.

"The doctor said you suffered a couple of broken ribs and a head injury that put you in a mild coma."

Whoever did this to me would feel my revenge big-fucking-time. I wanted their head on a silver platter. Monica told me to relax, and even though I wanted to fuck a bitch up, I couldn't do anything about it because the medicine kicked in and knocked a bitch flat on her ass.

# Chapter 22

## Monica

### Three Weeks Later

The weather was steaming and extremely hot. You could cook an egg on the pavement. My agenda was simple today—Head to the hospital, pick Kiah up, take her shopping, and try to find out who hit her and left her to die. Whoever it was best believe they were going to feel my wrath storming down on them. I grabbed my business phone to check and see if The Voice had something for me. The money that I was making had me set for life.

As I stared at myself in the mirror, I took a few pictures before posting them on my Instagram. I had on a pair of Levi's, a Ralph Lauren fitted shirt that showed my girls off very well, and some Ralph Lauren open-toed sandals. I searched for my other phone and noticed I had six missed calls. There were three from Marcus, and the other three were from Kim. *I wonder what they wanted,* I thought to myself. I did miss Marcus. I hadn't seen him in weeks. I hadn't been taking his calls either. Kim had been blowing up my phone trying to talk about her relationship trouble which I didn't give a fuck about.

*RING! RING!*

"Hello?" I answered in a curious tone, trying to detect the caller's voice because I didn't know the number.

"Girl, if you don't stop changing your voice," Kiah said, laughing in the background.

"What you up to, boo?"

"I'm outside. Open up." Kiah laughed.

I grabbed my personal belongings, and as I was opening the door, Kim was attempting to knock. I caught her hand in midair. I knew I had spooked her by the expression on her face.

"Hey, girl!" I said.

"I was just trying to surprise you today."

She gave me a girly hug. Kim was rocking a Klay Thompson jersey and khaki shorts. She had hair down to her shoulders. The texture of her hair was not like most black women. I asked her if she was mixed with something. She claimed that she wasn't.

"You did that!" I chuckled and closed the door behind me.

"Where you headed to?" she asked.

"'Bout to go pick up my sister from the hospital," I responded, dropping my hater blockers on my eyes because the sun wasn't playing.

"I didn't know you had a sis," she said.

"Naw, I don't. She's not my blood. She's my best friend."

I filled her in on me and Kiah's relationship. She just nodded, saying she understood.

"Would you like to ride?" I asked as I headed to the car because I already had beads of sweat trailing down my forehead.

"Sure," she said.

When we stepped outside, I noticed that she was driving in something new. I was about to comment on it, but my phone started to vibrate. It indicated that I had a text message. It was Marcus. He was letting me know that he needed to talk to me. I just threw the phone back into my bag and jumped in the car as we headed to pick up Kiah.

## Chapter 23

### Marcus

*BANG! BANG!*

My partner burst into my office with a deranged facial expression and some photos of the previous night's homicide.

"What up?" I said, standing up from behind the desk. She didn't respond; she just dropped off the caseload and proceeded on about her business. I was about to stop her, but I wasn't up for a debate over my personal life, so I figured I would deal with her once I found these wannabe serial killers.

The photos of the victim revealed that he was shot numerous times in the torso. The body was discovered at the victim's residence around 3:00 a.m. *What was happening in my small city that's causing the murder rate to increase in the last six months?* I thought to myself.

Right before I was about to make a call, I got a page from Chief Bryant that he wanted to see me in his office. I covered my face with both of my hands because it felt like my life was shifting downward at this point. *What could possibly be fucking next?* I said in my head.

The door of the chief's office was slightly ajar, so I entered the office and saw that he was on the phone. He made a hand gesture for me to have a seat.

*Ain't this some bullshit. How is he going to page me and not be ready?* I thought to myself. I could tell he was heated by the expression on his face. I could see the wrinkles form on his beet-red face. I could tell he was getting his ass chewed out by whoever was on the other end of the phone. Nine times out of ten, he was going to chew me out. That's how things work.

"Bastard!" the chief shouted into the phone, then he slammed his hand on his desk, causing his pictures to fall. I caught one of them and placed it back on his desk.

"Thanks, kid," he said, sipping a clear substance from his cup.

"You alright?" I asked as he grabbed some paper towels to wipe the sweat off his forehead. Chief Bryant and I had some history. He showed me the ends and outs around the force. Without him, I would not be the man that I was. He took another sip then looked at me.

"What is the move?" I asked, wondering what the meeting was about.

"You're the fucking problem. That's the move!" he shouted, slamming his fist on the surface of his desk. I was about to speak, but he was on fire. "I don't know what the hell is going on around here. Too many people are coming up dead and no arrests. That's not like you!" he yelled as spit came flying directly in my face.

Chief was right. Things weren't right around the department.

"Chief, I've been working overtime to find the suspects," I pleaded my case to let him know I was putting in work, but the killer had not left any evidence behind.

"Chief, I'm—"

He cut me off. "Marcus, you better hit the streets and find out quick before you come up missing," he threatened.

His hand gesture let me know that he wanted me to exit his office. He was as hot as a firecracker that was about to explode at any minute.

"Chasing love will keep you unbalanced," he said, waving me out of his office.

I stood on the other side of the door empty and confused. He's right. I was very distracted. I was trying to get Monica to fall for me and wasn't putting my all into solving these cases.

I proceeded out the door and took a detour to my

partner's office. She was not present, so I walked toward her desk. I noticed her desk drawer was ajar and a small device was visible. I quickly examined it. It was a voice decoder.

"What the hell is she doing with this?" I said to myself.

I placed it back where I found it and went straight to my office and pulled out my phone. I tried to call my partner. The phone rang twice, then it went to the voicemail. I left one message and told her to get at me as soon as possible.

Something weird was going on around me, but I just couldn't put my finger on it. Scanning through the files that were stacked on my desk, I tried to find any type of evidence that would lead me to solve this mystery. As I searched for anything, my efforts were becoming pointless. My frustration was building up. I slung everything off my desk. The pressure was too much, and I couldn't take it anymore. I grabbed my keys and jetted. I had to get to the bottom of this.

# Chapter 24

## Zykiah

The sunlight peered through the slightly parted blinds of the hospital room, forcing my eyes to struggle with blurred vision. I couldn't wait to leave this sick place. I'd been gone from the streets too long. The doctors were about to run the last test to make sure everything was on point before I could leave. They needed to hurry the fuck up because this place was about to drive me insane. A few moments later, the door flew open, and I quickly snapped out of my trance.

The nurse was coming to get me to run some tests. I tried to walk myself, but they wouldn't allow it as they rolled me around to the test department

"Everything is good, Ms. Harris," the doctor said while he pulled me out of the CAT scan machine.

He was a middle-aged man with a dark skin complexion. He was African with a deep voice that made goosebumps appear all over my body. I couldn't wait until Aubrey came back in town because a bitch needed some sexual healing. The other nurse rolled me back into the room and brought release papers for me to sign. They prescribed me medication for my pain as well.

I headed to the bathroom to get ready for my departure and took a shower. The lukewarm water hit the side of my body and all my tension was released. As I was about to get out, I heard voices in the other room. I quickly put on my clothes. I knew that Monica was coming to pick me up. Finally, after I was all dressed, I headed to the door. As I pushed the door open, I noticed that the voices I heard belonged to Monica and some other woman.

"Heyyyyy!" Monica said as she rushed to greet me with a loving hug. She damn near squeezed the life out of me.

"Mo… ohhhh!" I groaned out because the hug sent pain through my body.

"Ohhh! I'm sorry!" she said as she realized I was still injured. She kissed my cheek apologetically.

"Oh, Kiah, I almost forgot. I want you to meet somebody," she said then pointed in the direction of this mystery woman.

As she turned around, our eyes connected, and it was very awkward. A strange feeling ran through my veins.

"This is my sister, Zykiah. Zykiah, this is Kim," Monica introduced us.

I reached my hand out to shake hers, and Kim extended hers out to receive mine. There was something about this woman that gave me a bad vibe, but I couldn't put my finger on it. I was a good person at reading people very well. I gave her a polite smile, but her body language let me know that she must've felt how I was feeling because she did the same thing.

Monica helped me gather my belongings, then we headed out of the hospital. I felt so excited to leave. The bright sun shined directly in my eyes. Monica pulled some Dolce shades from her bag and gave them to me. Once I put the shades on my eyes, I could endure the brightness. We headed to her whip. The parking garage was packed. As we walked through the garage, we came upon a whip that I didn't recognize. Monica was pushing a Bentley Mulsanne. It was pearl-white with chrome rims. My girl was stunting on these hoes.

"Nice!" I complimented, wiping off of her shoulder like Jay-Z.

She hit the alarm. I opened the door on the passenger side and jumped in.

"I'll be damned!" I said as I sat back in the seat.

The inside was peanut butter with white stitching. My girl had her name engraved on the seats. I gave her a wink and said, "Bitch, you did that!"

She started the engine. The blizzard air conditioning caused chill bumps to appear on my arms immediately. Tamia's "Can't Get Enough" was erupting from the speakers. I closed my eyes as I began thinking about Aubrey and his hands all over my body.

"Girl, what's wrong with you?" Monica asked me. It suddenly brought me out of my sexual daydream. "You over there cheezin' like you having some twisted thought."

"To be honest with you, I can't wait until my man comes back into town."

The thoughts had me wanting to caress my pussy through the tights I had on.

"What kind of work he do, Zykiah, if you don't mind me asking?" Kim questioned.

"He's a truck driver," I responded.

"Okay. Truck drivers have shaky relationships," she added.

"And?" I shot back. That black bitch didn't even know me, and she was trying to give me some relationship advice.

"I'm just saying… They live so many lives. I'm married to a truck driver, and that motherfucker stays cheating," she said like I gave a fuck about her.

"Well, if you still with him and he's still cheating on you, that tells a lot about *you*!" I said with emphasis.

I was never the one to bite my tongue for any bitch.

"Woahhh!" Monica jumped in because the tension had built up. She must have felt it because I was ready to jump across the seat. There was something I didn't like about that pussy ass hoe.

"We good, Mo! I was just saying' some real shit. I didn't mean to offend her, but I can't see myself knowing my man is cheating, and I ain't doing shit about it."

We all were silent the whole ride until we made it to our destination. We arrived at the Albany Mall. We shopped all the department stores and made about two or three trips to the car because we couldn't carry all the bags. After we were done, we stopped by my favorite ice cream shop, and I got a waffle cone with chocolate chip cookie dough ice cream. Monica got chocolate ice cream on a regular cone, and Kim was acting all prissy. She didn't eat anything. She said she was on a diet. I just smirked at her. She had a nice body, but it was nothing like mine.

Twenty minutes later, we arrived at Monica's condo. She pulled up next to a money green Audi A8. I was exhausted; the sun had drained all the energy out of me. Monica and I said our goodbyes to Kim, and I grabbed most of my bags while she collected the rest.

"Woo!" I said, flopping down on the loveseat. I was glad the air was on. I had sweat all down my back. Monica went to the kitchen to grab some refreshments.

"Thanks," I said, gobbling down a Hi-C. I was instantly ready for some more.

"You must have been thirsty, girl," she said while refilling my cup with some pink stuff.

"I'm glad you're back because I was missing you," she expressed with a girlie hug.

It brought tears to my eyes. We sat there and had a crying session until the sound of Plies' "Murder Season" ringtone started blasting.

"Yeah, what's the MUU?" Monica asked with a different tone in her voice, so I knew business had just come up.

She wiped her tears and headed to the bathroom. Within seconds, she came out looking like midnight all over.

"Gotta go handle some business, Kiah," she informed me.

I just threw my hands up.

"Just come back to me, bitch," I commanded.

She rushed over and gave me a big hug.

"Mo, I don't like Kim," I said.

"I can tell. Don't worry about nothing. I got you," she assured me.

She closed the door. She was gone within minutes. I sat on the couch channel surfing, trying to find something to watch. I finally settled on the first season of *Empire*.

"That girl, Cookie, is my bitch." I watched *Empire* until my eyes started getting heavy.

# Chapter 25

## Monica

It was pitch dark outside. I lay ducked down behind the steering wheel as I waited for the perfect time to strike. I'd been out here for the past hour. I checked my inventory to ensure everything was ready. The vehicle I was waiting for had just pulled up. The guy was driving an old beat up Ford truck. The driver was a stocky ass nigga. I watched as he went to the passenger side, grabbed a duffel bag, and disappeared into the house. The living room lit up then immediately got dark.

I grabbed all my gear and looked in the small mirror to adjust the black wig that hung over my shoulders. Approaching the front door, I knocked softly until he opened it. Up close, he was not big but not small either. He had a pot belly like he was a big beer drinker and had been drinking his whole life. He looked to be in his early fifties due to all the snow-white hair. He had the door cracked halfway and stared at me with lust in his eyes.

"May I help you, ma'am?" he asked, looking at my cleavage.

*This is going to be easy,* I thought.

"Sorry for disturbing you this time of night, but my car tire is flat, and my phone just died," I said with sorrow in my voice.

He immediately jumped on the opportunity.

"It's okay. We all go through something in life." He guided me inside.

The house was plain, and you could easily tell he stayed there alone. His living room furniture screamed for help, and his couch looked like it came off the set of *Good Times. I thought people had stopped using floor model TVs,* I thought to myself.

"You're welcome to call someone to come help you because I don't have a clue how to fix cars," he said with a smirk on his face.

*I'm going to wipe that smirk off his face, and he doesn't even know it yet.* He walked me toward the phone, I grabbed it and sat on the couch.

"Make yourself at home," he said and disappeared in the back.

I pretended like I was talking to someone when he came back into the room.

"Would you like something to drink?" he asked.

I didn't say anything; I just nodded my head. He came back with two glasses halfway full of some gin, so I figured he would try to get me drunk.

"Thanks for letting me use the phone." I smiled while grabbing the glass, faking like I was about to drink.

"No problem. Were you able to get in contact with someone?" he asked with "I hope not" written all over his face.

"Yeah, my best friend is coming," I lied.

"Do you have any chaser for this gin... like some Ruby Red juice?" I suggested.

He nodded and headed to the kitchen cabinet. While he was searching, I slipped out the powder substance, poured it into his drink, and watched it dissolve.

Once that got into his system, he would be out like a light. That would allow me to do what I was sent for. He walked back into the room with a confident smile like he just knew it was about to go down. Little did he know, it was not in his favor. Right before he sat down, the doorbell rang.

"Who the heck is that?" he said in an irritated voice.

He handed me the juice before walking toward the door.

"Who is it?"

"Marcus," the man responded.

Once I heard the name, the hairs on my neck stood

up. *This can't be him,* I thought to myself. If it was, I couldn't take any chances, so I looked at him and told him to get rid of him as I stuck my finger in my mouth. Whatever he had on his mind before that sealed the deal. He opened the door enough to allow him to put his head out. While he was getting rid of him, I ditched my drink just in case he put something in mine. I also confirmed that it was Marcus by peeping out the window. I thought he saw me because he kept staring at the blinds. The door closed, and he locked it ASAP and sat back on the couch, gazing at me with sex in his eyes.

"Back to what we were doing."

"Who was that guy if you don't mind me asking?"

"He's a guy I work with," he stated.

"What kind of work do you do?" I repositioned myself.

"I'm chief of police," he said.

My heart stopped for a split second. *The police chief?* I had to get my thoughts together. I had to make sure I didn't leave anything in his place or they would bury me under the prison. My palms started to get moist. "You okay, Ms…" he asked, snapping me out of my thoughts.

"Gina. Yes, I'm okay."

"Gina. That's a cute name."

"Thanks."

I gave a fake blush. He grabbed his cup and threw it back like it was going out of style. I refilled it some more. I sipped some out of my cup. He thought there was gin in mine, but I had more juice in mine. I had to kill time until the drugs kicked in, so I started rubbing his legs. I felt like I was about to vomit. He had wet, hairy, slimy thighs. He tried to unzip my pants.

"Let's go to the bedroom," I advised him.

We got halfway to the room, and I could tell it was time for me to say it was over with for him. He staggered, holding his head and rubbing his eyes. Once we made it to the room and onto the bed, he was completely out of it. I ran back to the living room and grabbed my bag. First, I handcuffed him to the bed. Then, I duct taped his mouth and taped his feet together. I took my camera out and took pictures. I pulled out this long, sharp razor blade and ripped his shirt right down the middle so that he had only his boxers on.

"Eww."

Nothing was amazing about his mini-sausage. It was time to handle business because I was not trying to be there all night. I took the blade, placed it at the top of his chest, and went straight down. His flesh ripped apart like fish skin. Blood sprayed out and soaked the sheets. I swiped the sharp blade straight across his neck. I detached his skull from his body and put it in the black duffel bag. It was crazy how one could be gone in the blink of an eye. I wasted no time. I collected everything I had touched and got the fuck out of there. I dropped the duffel bag off at the address that was texted to my phone and headed home. I was beyond disgusted.

# Chapter 26

## Marcus

Driving around, I still couldn't believe Chief Bryant had a lady at his house. I had a weird feeling in my gut telling me something wasn't right. *What can it be?* I asked myself that over and over again. I pulled out my iPhone and commanded it to call Monica. She picked up on the third ring.

"Hello."

She answered, breathing real heavy like she was running.

"You okay?" I asked because she sounded like she had a lot going on in her background. I heard a lot of movement and fidgeting with stuff. She still hadn't said anything yet, so I repeated myself.

"Yeah. Why you shouting in my fucking ear!" she yelled.

"Because I was trying to get with you tonight," I pleaded.

"I'm kinda busy right now."

"Just for five minutes."

"I don't know about that."

"Come on, Monica. Just give me a chance."

"Fine. Where do you want to meet?"

"Meet me at the BP gas station on the corner of Broad."

Ten minutes later, I pulled up at the gas station and spotted Monica parked under the BP sign. I pulled right beside her car, hopped out, and approached her door. She looked exhausted and sweat was all over her beautiful face.

"So, what you want to talk to me about?" She hurried and broke the ice.

"Monica, I miss you," I confessed, licking my lips.

"I hear you," she said with a sarcastic tone.

"Yeah. Every time I watch TV or listen to any kind of music, you're there. I can't stop thinking about you."

"I told you I'm—"

I cut her off. "I don't want to hear that sorry excuse about you ain't ready. I see how you look at me. So, don't I make you happy?" I asked, grabbing her hand.

I was giving it to her because I was serious about her. I had to pull out all the stops. She tried to speak, but I wouldn't allow her.

"Mo, I've been going crazy. I need you back in my life."

I stuck my head in the window and planted a wet, sloppy kiss on her lips. When I saw that she wasn't refusing, I knew I had my babe back. Our tongues played tag until her phone started to vibrate.

"Marcus, I'm not going to lie... I miss you as well. Just don't hurt me because I'm letting you in."

We sat there and talked about our future. I let her know things would be gravy. We kissed again. This time, I didn't close my eyes. I noticed she had a black wig in her car.

*What the fuck she got going on?* I thought to myself.

I wanted to ask her, but I had just gotten back in good, so that was out of the question.

We made it back to her condo. Before she could even step out the car, I was all over her. She was no different. She kissed me all over my neck as I pushed her up against the hood. She had wrapped her right leg around my waist, so I cupped her fat ass. She somehow unbelted my pants. She grabbed my dick. Her hands felt magnificent. She massaged the tip of my shit.

"Mmm," was all I could moan out.

The midnight stars shined right over our bodies. I took her to the front of the car, bent her over, and pulled down her pants. Her pussy was dripping wet. I had to taste it.

"Wooooo… sss…" she moaned out while my tongue attacked her pussy walls.

Her pussy was the best I had ever tasted.

"Damn, this shit good."

She pulled my head up and looked back at me.

"Damn, you're so beautiful," I told her, gazing at her.

"Give it to me, daddy," she said, begging for the dick.

I put my dick all inside of her. I stroked with precision and gripped her hair as I pounded my dick in and out of her pussy walls.

"Shit… This dick good."

"You miss this dick?" I kept picking up speed.

"Ye-yes… yesss!"

"Yeah, what?" I demanded her to say it.

"I miss this dick!" She was throwing that ass back like she was a pro.

"Take this dick!"

"Fuck this pussy!" she yelled out.

Why did she have to say those words? She had me so far gone. I thrust harder and harder. I spread her cheeks and got all in that good pussy.

"I'm cumming, Marcus!" she screamed, gripping the top of the hood tightly.

I shot everything I had in me into her. I carried her inside and lay her on the couch. I went back outside. Her phone started to vibrate again, so I just flipped it over. The text read *Mission well done.*

I was totally confused. I headed back into the house where she was sound asleep. I carried her into the bedroom. I laid in the bed, staring at the ceiling until I fell asleep. I continued to wonder what she had going on.

# Chapter 27

## Zykiah

### The Big Trip

I sprayed my entire body with strawberry cream body spray by Victoria's Secret and slid on my black lace Prada dress. I looked in the mirror and all I could say was, "Damn, I'm a bad bitch!" I ran my hand down the side of my body, grabbed my gold Tiffany necklace from the dresser, and put it on.

*RING! RING!*

"Hello?" I answered.

*CLICK!* The phone hung up in my face. This had been going on since I got out of the hospital. I just shook my head.

"Stupid ass bitches."

That's all I could say at that moment. I went straight to the cabinet and poured a small glass of Pineapple Cîroc.

"Yes!" I said, enjoying every drop.

*KNOCK! KNOCK!*

When I opened the door, there was a gentleman standing there in a very expensive Troy Ford suit and a dozen roses in his hand. He handed me the roses.

"Thank you."

Once I opened the door wider, I saw a stretch Escalade. It was bright purple. That was my favorite color. The gentleman opened the door, and Aubrey greeted me with a big, wet kiss.

"Hey, baby. I missed you," I told him.

"I missed you too."

He held me in his arms and kissed me uncontrollably. It felt so good to be in his presence again. I hadn't seen him in a long time since he had been on the road working.

As he took my hand, I followed him out toward the limousine and hopped inside.

I didn't even see Monica and Marcus cuddled up in the corner staring into each other's eyes.

"Damn, this limo is huge," I whispered.

I scooted down and gave Mo a hug while Marcus and Aubrey talked.

"What's the plan?" I asked with excitement.

"Well, first, we're going to cruise the town before we head out for the weekend to the finest resort in the world located in Miami," Aubrey whispered in my ear.

The limo was loaded with all kinds of liquor and brand name wines. Anything you could think of, the limo had it. It was like a mini-house. It had a bitch feeling famous. I didn't care how far we were going. I was just glad we were getting out of boring ass Albany for the week. We drank liquor and jammed to some music. A few hours later, we called it a night and headed back to my place where we all crashed so we could pick up our rental car in the morning.

The next morning, we all headed out to pick up our rental car. Monica reserved a Range Rover Land Rover S. We all loaded up inside the truck and headed out for our weekend destination. Finally, after a nine-hour ride, we arrived in the great city of Miami. The traffic was flooded with an assortment of cars. We saw cars sitting on huge rims. We even saw the Maxima on twenty-four inches.

"Damn, that bitch is nice. Y'all, look!" I said, and everybody looked and agreed that it was.

"Look at that fine ass paint job on that bitch," Aubrey said.

It was a candy-purple color with a powder purple interior. It was over the top. The streets were packed to the max.

I stuck my head out of the window and screamed at the top of my lungs, "Miami, baby!" The scenery was better in person than the advertisements. The sun was out shining really bright. I was totally amazed by some of the things I saw. This place is better than I imagined. We were on our way to an area in Miami called Liberty City where the infamous Pork & Beans projects stood. The first thing I thought of was the *First 48*.

We took 62nd Street to the MLK Boulevard exit and headed to go see my cousin Keevonya. She stayed in the Pork & Beans projects.

"Mo! This that spot where shit go down!"

Monica gave me a nod and said, "Mmhmm. Yes, girl!"

My phone started to vibrate, and a text came across my screen.

**Keevonya:** *Damn, cuz, are you here yet?*

**Me:** *Yes, boo. We on 62nd street right now in the Beans, about to turn on 15th Avenue. We'll be there in three minutes.*

When we pulled up, Keevonya was posted up on her porch. I hopped out the truck, ran up, and gave her the biggest hug. We held each other tight and jumped up and down. I hadn't seen my cousin in about six years, so I was glad we linked up. We walked back to the truck, and I introduced her to Aubrey and Marcus; She already knew Monica. They all hugged. Kee jumped in the truck with us, and we all went to eat dinner. Kee knew a perfect spot we could go to that was down the street. It was a restaurant called MLK. As we pulled up, cars were everywhere. Talk about Ms. Bessie's, this place had it going on. I saw police, correctional officers, business people, and street niggas who were sitting down and enjoying their food. We all walked in and grabbed a table. The waiter came over to greet us and gave us our menus. The food smelled so good it could wake up the dead.

As we sat there, I scanned my menu. I ordered steamed Tilapia with grits, and a side of salmon patties. Monica ordered smothered steak with mash potatoes and gravy

"Girl, don't hurt yourself, Ms. Greedy," I said.

We busted out laughing. Keevonya got the fried Tilapia with the same sides as me. Marcus got the smothered pork chops, with a side order of green beans and potatoes. Finally, Aubrey placed his order. He ordered a steak, French beans, and fries on the side.

As we waited for our food, people were in and out. It was like a trap house, but they were trapping food. They had the jukebox playing music while people were waiting and getting served. Finally, our food arrived.

"Oh my God," I said.

The dishes were prepared so wonderfully. I had never seen Tilapia fixed like this before. It was steamed in lemon juice with onions and bell peppers sliced over the top of it. It was served steaming hot. They all looked at my food and were impressed.

As we looked at each other, we all had the same agreement. Once everyone's food arrived, we all went in for the kill. The iced tea, orange juice, and fruit punch were swinging. Plus, they had this bread called Johnny Cakes. It was a dish the Bahamian people took pride in cooking. I didn't know who Johnny was, but those fucking cakes were like no other. That was the best bread I'd ever tasted.

"I sure wish we had a spot like this in Albany," I said to the crew.

They all agreed. We got so stuffed that we barely could fucking move. You can tell when food is good because it will have your body so relaxed to the point you'd be wanting to fall asleep.

"Keevonya, girl, thank you. We were due for a good meal."

"You're welcome," she said.

We headed on through the city. Kee became our tour guide. Our next stop was the famous USA flea market. As we were approaching the parking lot, I noticed it was packed like we were at a high-end place or something. The building was huge. Being from the country, our flea market wasn't anything close to this. We parked, jumped out, and headed to the entrance. On our way in, we saw food vendors throughout the parking lot.

We were not prepared for what we were about to see. There were booths everywhere. There was jewelry, shoes, clothes, electronics, pictures, barbers, and food vendors. We had never seen a flea market so upscale. They even had an area for the kids called Kiddie Land with a merry-go-round, games, and all kinds of entertainment for the kids. We were totally blown away by what we saw. Music was playing throughout the building. This place was a one-stop shop.

We all just fell in love. Aubrey and Marcus were too busy looking at the chicken head ass hoes walking around with tight ass clothes all up their asses. I had to admit that those Miami bitches surely had it. Those hoes were on fleek. They looked like they got out of their beds and got dressed to kill to go to the flea market.

"You never know who you might run into, so a bitch gotta always be on point. There are too many Roxy ass bitches out trying to slay you," Kee said.

Looking around, I could see she was right. We stopped at a bunch of booths and bought all types of stuff. Monica and I got these matching shirts that were airbrushed and had "Albany's Finest" sprayed on them. We got our hair bumped and got our nails and feet done at the same damn time. We were like two kids in a candy store, especially with all of the fine ass niggas that were up in this bitch. All we saw were dudes with long dreads and gold teeth with big Cuban chains on. We made our way to the jewelry booths. Kee knew a booth where we could get whatever we wanted.

"I'mma take y'all to Ms. B's booth," Kee said.

Ms. B was known by every dope boy and hustler in Miami that was getting money. She had a fine selection of jewelry. On top of that, she always had a deal for you. As we were walking up to the booth, Ms. B noticed Kee.

"Hey, child, what they do?" Ms. B asked.

Aubrey, Mo, and I were like "What the fuck? Did this Chinese lady just get ghetto?"

Our mouths dropped. Kee started laughing at us. Our faces were priceless.

Then, Ms. B said, "Hey, y'all, how can I help you today?"

Still amazed by the hood ass Chinese woman, we still

didn't speak.

"Y'all ain't from around here I see, but don't worry. I'mma fuck with y'all!"

We gagged at how hood she really was.

*Oh my God! It's like that in Miami? Wow!* I thought to myself.

Ms. B showed us all kind of shit, from five hundred to twenty bands. Aubrey bought a Cuban Link chain with a Jesus piece and a bracelet to match. Marcus also got a Cuban Link chain with a trippy Cuban Link bracelet. Monica and I got these big diamond nameplates with the Cuban Link chain and diamond name bracelet with a ring that had our names spelled out in diamonds. We had to wait a couple of hours before our stuff was ready.

"Bitch! Mo, Albany ain't gonna be ready for us when we get back. We gonna give it to them hoes like we always do," I said, then we gave each other a high five.

Keevonya looked in amazement as if to say, "Where the fuck y'all country ass folks get money from like that?" but she didn't say anything.

Being the boss bitch that I was, I hit her off with a stack so she didn't feel left out.

It was getting late, so we dropped Kee off and headed to our spot we had reserved at the Ritz-Carlton on South

Beach. On our way to the beach, we saw plenty of attractions. We passed by Star Island on our way over to South Beach. Star Island got its name because a lot of famous people lived on the island like Lil' Wayne and Shaq. We also passed by Parrot Jungle and saw the Carnival Cruise ship docked at the Port of Miami. We rode on I-195 until it came to an end.

"Wow, this has to be one of the best-looking places in the world."

I could see Mo and them looking amazed as they gazed out of the windows. We all were stunned. We saw everything from Lambos to Phantoms all over the place. People with nice bodies were everywhere. It was like a scene out of the movies. The weather was perfect for a nice evening. Cruising along Collins Avenue, we saw a lot of clubs, stores, people on scooters, and people walking the streets.

"I guess we came at the right time," I said out loud to everyone.

They nodded their heads in agreement.

Monica busted out laughing and said, "Sho did."

I just laughed at that fool because I knew she was ready to turn up Miami style and be as nasty as she wanted to be.

Aubrey yelled out, “Call Uncle Luke and tell him I’m in Miami, too!”

“Alright, Lil’ Drake,” Marcus said, and we all started laughing.

Finally, the navigation said, “You will arrive at your destination in three minutes.”

Boy, was I glad. As we were pulling up, I noticed plenty other nice hotels along the strip. Nothing was like the Ritz-Carlton. It was spectacular. I see what Plies was talking about. It was some boss ass shit.

*This is definitely for a boss bitch and her crew,* I thought to myself. We were met at the door by the concierge and the bellboys. They had everything laid out for us. It was like a dream come true. Our rooms were on the twenty-ninth floor. Aubrey and I had a penthouse suite that had a second floor and so did Monica and Marcus. Our rooms were side by side. We entered our rooms at the same time and vanished for the rest of the evening. I was indeed tired. I couldn’t wait to get undressed, hit the shower, and lay down. That was my plan, but Aubrey had a different plan in mind.

“Damn, babe. What’s up? You already know what time it is.”

“Huh?”

"It's Mr. Smash time," Aubrey responded.

We were already undressed. I was tired, but when it came down to fucking my man, I could've been drug by a car, but I still was giving up this pussy. As I lay down on the California king bed, Aubrey was all over me. He started licking my neck and made his way down to my pussy. The lower he went, the wetter I became. He spread my legs, and all I could do is lay there and enjoy the pleasure he had me feeling. He inserted his long tongue into my pussy, stroking and sucking it like it was the main course on his plate. The deeper he went with his tongue, the more turned up I got.

I grabbed his head and held it as tight as I could and screamed, "Eat this pussy, daddy!"

He stuck his middle finger in my ass. That shit had me cumming so hard that it ran all down my ass crack.

"Yes, daddy, make me cum for ya!" I yelled.

Next thing I know, he flipped me over and started hitting it from the back. He was smacking my ass and pulling my hair at the same time. He fucked me like he was a nigga fresh off the chain gang.

"Oh my God, his big dick ass was really working me over!" I said to myself.

I thought we were loud until I heard thumps coming

from next door. Mo and Marcus had to be getting it in too. After we had both reached our peak, I had to soak in the jacuzzi and let the water massage my body all over. After our shower together, Aubrey carried me to the bed. We held each other until we fell asleep.

*RING! RING!*

It was 12:30 a.m. My phone started ringing off the hook.

"Who the fuck is it?" I wondered.

The display read *Kee*.

"Hello?" I said, half asleep.

"Bitch, what y'all doing?" Kee said.

"Girl, we are in the bed."

"Oh, hell nah. Y'all get y'all asses up. We don't sleep in this city," she said.

Bitch, it's 12:30 a.m. Where we gonna go?"

"Bitch, really? Girl, the night just got started. We going to KOD tonight, so y'all get up and get ready. I'll call you back around 1:30 a.m., so be ready. Rick Ross and Trina will be in the building tonight. I'm having drinks at The Office right now. It's the other strip club next to KOD, so I'll be waiting on y'all. Later."

The phone went silent. I woke Aubrey's ass up. He was sleeping like a baby. Then, I called Monica and

Marcus to let them know what the move was for the night. She picked up sounding like she had been drugged.

"Sup, bitch?" Monica said.

"Girl, get your ass up," I demanded.

"It's 12:40 a.m., Kiah," Monica whined.

"Yes, girl, I know. You know this city don't sleep."

I informed her that Kee was inviting us out.

"She's already having drinks at the strip club called The Office. She's waiting for us."

"Okay, girl. Let me get my ass up because we didn't come here to sleep. Bitch, let's go turn up."

"Okay."

I hung up the phone and started getting ready. I picked up the phone and dialed room service. I was starving, and I knew Aubrey was too. I ordered a ten-ounce steak with a fully loaded baked potato, corn on the cob, and some fresh cheese biscuits. I got Aubrey the lamb chops with red potatoes made with parsley, garlic, and chives, and a side of creamy spinach with some fresh bread. I also got us a bottle of Moët. We finished getting dressed while we waited for our food to arrive. I texted Monica to let them know to do the same that way we didn't have to stop to get any food and could just head straight to the club from the Ritz.

Our food finally arrived. We sat at the table like a romantic couple on a first date. We ate and fed each other. We almost got caught up in the moment. Then, I realized it was getting late, and we had to go. We finished our food, cleaned ourselves up, and headed out. Mo and Marcus met us as we were walking out of the door.

"Damn, Mo. Girl, you ready to slay!" I said.

"Hell yeah, girl. Ross, Trick, and Plies are gonna be in the building tonight, so I had to go all out," Monica replied. "Girl, you ain't about to play either."

"Sure ain't, bitch. Trina and Jacki-O are gonna be there, so I'm trying to upstage them bitches and show them how an ole country ass bitch rocks!" I replied.

We burst out laughing. Aubrey and Marcus looked straight like money. It's easy to spot a tourist in Miami but not tonight. We picked up that Miami swag overnight and were ready to slay the city just like the local jokers. Marcus and Aubrey fit the typical Miami dope boy look with their Cuban Link chains on. All they were missing was the gold teeth.

We got on the elevator and headed to the main lobby. I had the truck detailed earlier that night while we were asleep. As we got down to the lobby, the concierge greeted us and led us to the Range Rover. It was parked in front waiting for us. As we got closer to the exit, the truck pulled up. The valet attendant hopped out and opened all four doors. As we got in, he closed every one of them and said, "Have a nice night."

"Thank you," I replied and rolled down my window to give him a hundred-dollar tip.

"Thank you, ma'am."

I headed down Collins Avenue toward I-395 to head back through the city. I put the address to King of Diamonds in the navigation system and followed the route. Once we connected to I-95, we drove through the city en route to KOD. Miami was beautiful at night with the lights, cars, and buildings. It was everything you could ever want out of the city life. Fifteen minutes later, we could see the strip and the parking lot. It was packed. Cars were all over the place. We even saw golf carts giving people rides to their cars. I called Kee to let her know we were in the parking lot.

Kee picked up and said to follow the road to the back of the building and I'd see KOD. She said she'd already be in line. I pulled up to the door. We got out and let the valet take it from there. Kee was in the line jumping up and down and waving, trying to get our attention. Finally, we saw her and jumped in the line with her. As I looked around, all I could see were niggas and hoes stunting from left to right. A lot of them were killing those loud ass colored clothes and shoes. Monica and I were amazed. These motherfuckers were dressed to kill, and I mean KILL.

*Damn, I gotta be in heaven all these fine ass Miami niggas,* I thought to myself.

I could see the same expression on Monica's face. I wished we had come here alone. Lord knows Aubrey and Marcus were so turned up they weren't paying us any attention. They were checking out every bitch that passed by. I know once we get in they were about to act a whole ass.

Finally, the line was moving, and we were at the door. Monica, Kee, and I went one way to get searched, and Aubrey and Marcus went the other way.

"Fifty dollars," the lady at the door said in regard to the entry fee.

"What?" I mumbled.

I didn't wanna seem like a petty broke bitch, but damn, fifty dollars to get up in this bitch? I'd never paid more than five dollars to get in a club, and the drinks were free. No pressure, though. We're in Miami, so it was cool. We didn't come to make it rain; we came to make a thunderstorm. We headed in.

Aubrey and Marcus were right behind us, looking lost. I tapped Aubrey on his shoulder.

“Bae, how much did y’all have to pay to get in?” I questioned.

“A hundred,” Aubrey said.

“Whew!”

“Let’s turn the fuck up!” I yelled.

The first thing we did was head up to VIP. We got a table and ordered four bottles of Cristal. I reached into my purse and gave the waiter the money, and we started pouring it up. Bitches were climbing from the fucking ceiling and hanging upside down. We saw strippers on poles and standing on top of each other. What really fucked us up was one stripper was crawling across the roof with another stripper on her back twerking her ass. It was wild. Aubrey and Marcus just lost it. Mo and I looked on in total amazement. I wasn't into hoes, but these bitches were fine as a motherfucker.

“Money in the building!” someone yelled out.

I turned to Kee and asked what that was all about.

Kee said, “That means we got some big spenders in the house.”

We all got a stack out and started tossing cash over

the rail in VIP. It looked like it was snowing five-dollar bills. Marcus and Aubrey excused themselves and went down the stairs in the VIP section. They said they were going to the bathroom.

"Yes, God. We got a break, so let's see what these Miami niggas talking about," Mo joked.

The VIP was packed to the max. Ross, Trina, Plies, Trick, and Jacki-O were present along with a lot of big-time dope boys and hustlers. Kee knew all of them. Monica and I politely walked through VIP to check out the scene as the niggas and bitches looked on.

One dude with dreads down his back stopped Kee and said, "Damn, Kee. Who is that you got with you?"

"Oh, just my cousins from Georgia," Kee answered as he was getting closer to us.

"Oh, y'all from Georgia, huh?" the dread head asked.

I just nodded my head.

"So, lil' mama, what part of the A y'all from?"

"Nope! Albany," Monica said and put a little neck into it.

"What's your name, Ms. Lady?" the dread head questioned.

"My name is Kiah."

Before I could utter another word, I was cut off.

"Oh, my name is Innocence," Mo replied quickly.

"So, what y'all getting into tonight?" the dude said.

"Hold up. Why you ain't tell us your name?" I asked.

"Oh shit. My bad. My name is Budda."

We both stared at him. He was about six feet two, 195 pounds, and toned. He had a brown-skinned complexion with tattoos and a beard like Rick Ross. He had a mouth full of gold teeth with about three thick sized Cuban Link chains and a thick Cuban Link bracelet. He looked like Camion Marley but more wicked.

I stared because he was fine as a motherfucker.

"Here's my number if y'all tryin' to really see how we get down. I'll show y'all how we do it in the bottom."

I put his number in my phone. I knew I wasn't going to call, but I'd keep it for future reference. We headed downstairs in the midst of the crowd. This place was a damn strip club and a nightclub. Rick Ross and Trina were performing, and the crowd was dancing like hell. I saw people popping pills, hitting lines, smoking weed, and all kind of shit. We passed a couple of niggas who were smoking, but the smell was very unusual for it to be weed.

"Kee, what the fuck is that them niggas smoking?" I asked curiously.

"Oh, girl, you don't know? That's them damn boonke joints."

"Girl, what the fuck is that?" I questioned.

"It's weed and coke."

"You mean weed and cocaine together?" I asked.

"Yup… or a chopper."

"Girl, a what?"

"Cigarettes and cocaine… that's a chopper."

"They got it going on with that shit. I thought it was damn crack."

"Nah, when they do that, it's called geekin'. That's when you crush the crack up and smoke it in your joint or cigarette."

"Girl, nooo," I replied.

The crowd was partying like there was no tomorrow. I see why they said the city didn't sleep. It was 4:00 a.m., and this bitch was going in. People were still at the door trying to get in.

"Mo, girl, you see this shit here?"

"Girl, we can't hang with these damn folks. They're out of our league." I laughed because she was right.

"We damn sure ain't gonna act like it tonight," I said, and we all laughed.

We were looking to see if we could spot Marcus and

Aubrey when suddenly, the crowd went crazy. Plies hit the stage. At that moment, Mo and I forgot about Aubrey and Marcus. We were trying to see Plies. We made our way through the crowd and were in front of the stage.

Damn, Plies looked so good in person. The only thing was he was short as hell, but he was still cute, though. He was rapping and ran off on the plug twice. I grabbed a handful of money and slung it in the crowd. Mo threw some toward the stage. The club was going wild. Niggas were all up on a bitch's ass trying to get a feel on. Plies jumped off the stage and came over to me. Suddenly, I heard Akon's voice coming out the speaker.

"You got me so hypnotized that way your body moving 'round and 'round." The beat dropped. Plies grabbed me with one hand and had the mic in the other hand and went in.

"It's 2:00 in the morning. I'm jacked up, and I'm horny," he rapped. Oh my God, I lost it. I damn near broke my hip shaking my ass. Kee and Mo were hyping it up.

"Aye, aye!" Mo and Kee yelled out.

We had a blast. Plies finally returned to the stage, and Jacki-O came out. I was not too familiar with her, but I'd heard some of her music before. I tapped Mo.

"This bitch finna go in," I said all hyped up.

The niggas were standing all on top of the tables and money was flying in the air. We all looked to see where it was coming from. That's when we saw Aubrey and Marcus's asses on top of one of the bars. They both had duffle bags. They were grabbing money out of them and causing a thunderstorm.

"Mo, look at them damn fools."

"The fuck they think they are?"

We fell out laughing.

"They gonna get us robbed," I joked.

We finally linked back up, and we all agreed that it was time to go. We had the time of our lives. We all thanked Kee for the good time she showed us. All of us headed for the exit. I gave the valet my ticket so he could bring the truck around. Kee stood there until the truck pulled up. We all gave her a huge group hug and said our goodbyes.

"Kee, where you on your way to?" I questioned.

"Oh, to this after-hours spot called Lady Luck. It's a couple of exits away. Why? What's up? Y'all fucking with it?"

"Nah, cuz, we gotta get some rest before we hit the road," I told her.

It was 5:45 a.m., and these people were still trying to find the next spot to party.

"Well, cuzzo, see you next time!" I waved and drove off.

On my way back to the Ritz, the truck was silent. Monica was texting somebody. Her facial expression told me that something was not right. I didn't let it phase me. Everyone else was knocked out. I could tell that they were tired. We never partied like this before in our lives. I couldn't wait to hit the bed. I woke them up when we pulled up at the Ritz-Carlton. They looked like they didn't want to move, so I hit the brakes real hard and everybody jumped. That definitely woke their asses up. We finally made it our rooms and crashed out on the bed.

****

I stretched my arms as I sat up on the bed. This weekend had went by fast as hell. The whole weekend we partied every night and slept part of the day. I slick wanted to stay longer, but I knew that wasn't possible. It was time to head back home. I looked over at Aubrey and heard him snoring loud as hell. He was sounding like a damn freight train. I shook him and began to wake up.

"Good afternoon, babe," I greeted him.

He gave me a puzzled look.

"Afternoon, huh?" he said, sounding confused.

"Yep, babe, it's around 2:30 p.m."

"We slept this late, knowing we gotta get on the road?" Aubrey questioned.

I nodded my head. I picked up the phone to call Monica's room. She picked up on the fourth ring.

"Hello?" she answered.

"Bitch, get up. Girl, do you see what time it is?"

She got silent.

"Oh, shit!" Mo yelled.

"Girl, let's get it," I said and hung up.

Aubrey was in the shower already, so I joined him. We both started washing each other, and I noticed he was rock hard. All I could think about was him jamming that dick up in me. I snapped out of that trance when I noticed that Aubrey was getting out the shower. Damn, I really wanted some, but I knew we didn't have time to do a movie because that's what it was going to be.

I finished washing and dried off. Aubrey was damn near ready, and he was packing his things. I got myself together and started grabbing my things as well.

Once we were done and packed up, I called to make a reservation for four in their five-star restaurant that was located on the first floor of the hotel. We all left our rooms, got on the elevator, and headed for the lobby. The bellboys rolled our luggage to the truck while we went to the restaurant. On our way to the restaurant, it looked like the South Beach strip on Ocean Drive, but we were still inside the Ritz-Carlton. It was to die for. Going through the door, it had an elegant look. Soft music was playing, and it was very romantic. The host led us to our table with our menus. Aubrey and Marcus pulled out our chairs. Monica and I enjoyed that little moment. We all sat down and picked up our menus to see what they had to offer. I was hungry as hell. I got the shrimp and lobster fettuccine alfredo, garlic bread, and a sweet tea to drink. I also got a slice of chocolate cheesecake for my dessert.

Once everyone else noticed I wasn't playing, they started ordering their food. Mo got fried Red Snapper, Spanish rice, tossed salad, and some plantains with a slice of German chocolate cake. Aubrey got the baby back ribs with baked beans, potato salad, and a slice of red velvet cake. Marcus got the Surf and Turf. It consisted of a sixteen-ounce T-bone steak, fried shrimp seasoned with

Old Bay, Spanish rice, and red potatoes.

Our food came, and we pigged out. The food deserved ten stars; that's how good it was. Everything was perfect. When we got done, we pitched in on the tip. The waiter we had was very professional and down to earth. We had to show her some love. I put a fifty on the table and Monica did also. Aubrey and Marcus both put seventy-five a piece on the table. We thanked her for her hospitality. Her facial expression was priceless.

Next, we headed to the lobby. We stepped into the gift shop and bought T-shirts that said, *Ritz-Carlton, Miami South Beach 2016.* It was a little souvenir to remind us of our lovely stay. The bellboys had already placed our luggage and our bags in the back of the truck. I rolled my window down like I did last time and handed him $200. He hesitated to take it. He was very nervous to the point that when he grabbed the money, he almost dropped it. I made sure he had it before I drove off.

I passed down Collins and headed to Ocean Drive. I had to get a few more couple of pictures by the water. I parked, and we walked the strip for a good hour, taking pictures of everything. Our best picture was of the Gianni Versace mansion. We flicked it up to the max. We stopped by Fat Tuesday's to grab us a drink. They had tons of frozen drinks such as the Call a Cab, Superman, and a drink called DUI. We selected our drinks of choice and walked back in the other direction once we got them. We took several more pictures after we made it back to the truck. We saw a couple walking by and asked them if they could take a group picture of us. They agreed.

I gave the couple my phone to take the picture. She did a countdown then snapped the picture. We all thanked them, got into the truck, and headed toward I-95 North to the Florida Turnpike.

I screamed, “Goodbye Miami! Back to boring, country ass Georgia. Here we go!”

# Chapter 28

## Monica

"Wooo!" I said, stretching my arms out to get all the morning sleep out of my body. I had a blast in Miami. The Kind of Diamonds was turnt. That spot was like no other in the world. I'd always remember those exotic strippers. Those hoes really had skills. The Miami Beach water was beautiful and clear. I posted everything I saw on Instagram. We even took pictures in front of Gianni Versace's mansion. The only thing I still couldn't get over was the conversation I had with Kim. How could this woman be such a trifling hoe? I still couldn't believe that she was married to Aubrey. Aubrey was walking around like he was just so innocent, but this nigga was married.

How was I going to break the news to Zykiah and let her know the truth about her future husband? I bet it was Kim who put her in the hospital.

"Mmm… Good morning, beautiful," Marcus said while turning over and placing a small kiss on my lips.

"Ewww," I teased him about his morning breath.

"That's how you gonna do me?"

"Nah, I'm just playing," I said, kissing him back.

Marcus and I kicked it off good these last couple of days. The one thing I loved was how he and Zykiah interacted with each other. I saw that he could hold his own with her, so I knew he was a keeper.

"What's wrong with you, babe?" he asked.

He must have read my facial expression.

"Oh, nothing. I was just thinking about something."

"Like?" he questioned.

"It's a woman's thing," I replied.

He didn't press the issue, and I was grateful.

"What's our plans for today?" he asked curiously.

"My plan is to get some more rest because I'm drained," I said.

"Mm, we did wild out this weekend. Kiah is a real character," he said, sitting up in the bed.

"Yeah, she's been like that all her life."

Marcus just smiled at me with his pearly whites. My body was so out of it, but I would always remember that weekend. The Ritz-Carlton was a place I could live. While Marcus was in the bathroom, I texted Zykiah to let her know I would be over later that day. While I was sending that text, Marcus's phone was lighting up but not ringing.

"Why he got his phone on silent?" I asked myself.

My sirens went off, so I glanced over at the screen, and it read *Work.*

"Marcus, yo' phone ringing, baby!" I yelled over the music playing. The phone stopped then started back up, so I just grabbed it and took it to him. I opened the door. My eyes were locked on his six-pack. He stood there brushing his teeth. He looked so sexy. My nipples got hard as a brick. Damn, I want to eat this man up. I stood there for a split second until I realized the reason I came in there

"Baby, your job just called you."

"Thanks," he said and kissed me on my lips. I walked off and hopped back into my bed. My pussy was on fire! I just needed some early morning medicine. While he was in there getting himself together, I couldn't take it anymore. I spread my legs just a little and ran my two magic fingers down to my clit and went back and forth.

"Ssss," I moaned out. All I could imagine was his tongue gripping my pussy. I slid both fingers inside and dug all the way in. I was in the right groove.

"Shit!"

This time, my moan was loud, and I dug deeper until that white cream covered my fingers. I laid there and stared at the ceiling until I heard Marcus walk into the room.

"What? I'll be down right away."

Whoever he was talking to must have given him some upsetting news because his face was all balled up.

"Marcus, you okay?" I questioned.

Silence.

Marcus sat on the end of the bed with his face in his hands. Tears were running down his face. When he finally lifted his head up, I wondered what the fuck was going on with him.

"Marcus, what's going on?" I asked while caressing his hand.

"I… I… just found out that someone murdered my boss," he cried out.

Tears fell down his face like raindrops.

"I'm sorry to hear that," I said.

"Thanks. They said they've been trying to call me all weekend, but I had my phone on silent so I could enjoy my weekend with you," he confessed.

That confirmed my suspicion about him doing something.

"He died this weekend?" I questioned.

"Nah, the coroner said it was prior to that."

"Oh, man," I responded.

"They didn't have to do him like that."

"Like how, bae?" I asked with concern.

He just continued soaking in his tears. I felt so bad for him. I didn't want him going through this. Marcus was a great guy.

"Whoever killed him, zip-tied him and split him down the middle."

When he said that, his words tore through my body. I felt really horrible. He couldn't be talking about the same dude. He pulled out his phone. I thought he was about to place a call, but I was wrong. He swiped through his photos.

"This is me and him with this huge catfish I was telling you about," he said, wiping the tears out of his eyes.

I examined the picture closely. Once I saw his face, my mind went back to that awful night. *What have I done? I am a murderer.* I got silent. I didn't respond and only nodded my head. Marcus put his clothes on and gave me a passionate kiss, letting me know he would hit me up once he got things on the right path. Once I heard his car going down the street, I grabbed my other phone and contacted The Voice to let whoever they were know that I was done with killing. I got no response. I really didn't give a fuck.

## Later That Day

The neighborhood that Kiah had just moved into was really upscale. When I pulled up in her driveway, I shut my engine off as I gave myself the pep talk that I needed to walk into the house and tell her the truth about her man. It was time I told her the truth about Aubrey because she deserved to know what she was dealing with. After I had gotten up the courage to handle my business, I proceeded to the front door.

*BUZZ! BUZZ!*

She opened the door with a smile on her face. She still had on her night clothes. I could tell she probably had just had sex. Once she saw my face, she knew something was wrong. Her face changed immediately. I did my regular greet with a hug. We sat down on her Italian, cocaine white sofa. I grabbed her hand and looked into her eyes.

"What's wrong, Mo? You scaring me now."

"Where's Aubrey at?" I whispered. She pointed upstairs.

"Well, you remember when I told you I stopped by

the DMV?"

She looked to the sky, and then it hit her because she said, "Yeah!"

I repositioned myself in the chair.

"Well, I was just so lucky to be standing by Jihad's mistress."

"And?"

"The mistress is Kim," I said.

She looked confused. It was not adding up to her.

"I know you're wondering why I'm cool with her, but I was waiting for the right time to fuck that hoe up."

I placed my hand on hers and took a deep breath because I knew that what I was about to tell her was going to tear her world up.

"Kim is married to Aubrey."

Kiah's face got fiery-red. I knew I was hallucinating, but I thought I saw horns pop up.

"This can't be, Mo," she cried out.

I grabbed her head, brought it to my chest, and let her know things will be okay.

"Mo, I love you, but before you handle that bitch, wait on me."

I knew what was on her mind this time. I didn't refuse her.

"Okay, Kiah. I love you. Now, go handle your business."

I slid her the silencer from my purse as I closed the door behind me.

# Chapter 29

## Zykiah

*I can't believe this shit,* I thought to myself. I headed to the mini bar, grabbed a bottle of Cîroc, and gulped it down like it was nothing. I tucked the gun behind my back and went into the bedroom. When I stepped into the room, Aubrey was laid back like a king, looking at SportsCenter. They were showing Lebron James' NBA highlights from over the years. He waved for me to come over to where he was laying at.

I walked to the side of the bed and gave him a kiss. He tried pulling me on the bed, but I put my arms up to prevent him from doing so. While I was climbing in the bed, I instructed him to cover his eyes. When he closed his eyes, I slid the gun under the other pillow, slid off my night shorts, and straddled him as I looked him in the face.

"Mmm, babe," he moaned as I rotated my hips in a circular motion.

"Damn, bae, fuck this dick!" he yelled while gripping my ass cheeks.

It felt so good. I must admit, Aubrey had some good

dick. I popped my ass up and down. I knew he couldn't handle that. My pussy juices were slinging everywhere. I was fucking the hell out of his dick.

"Kiah... Zykiah, I'm about to nut."

His speed increased. I moaned loudly when he filled me up with his cum.

When he laid back with his eyes closed, I reached under the pillow to grab the gun. I put it behind my back and stepped off the bed.

"Aubrey, can I ask you something?" I asked.

"Anything, bae."

He rose up.

"Who is Kim?" I politely asked him.

His face had a perplexed look on it. I just stared at him with a look that said, "I already know, so come clean."

"Let me explain... please."

He tried to come my way, but I revealed what I had behind my back. He quickly came to a halt and raised his hands. Tears were running down my face. Once I felt the tears fall, I was enraged. I just wanted to blast a hole through his heart.

"Don't shoot me," he begged.

"Why not? You didn't give a fuck about me when you

were lying, so why should I give one now?"

"I love you, Zykiah," he confessed with tears filling his eyes.

"No the fuck you don't, Aubrey! You're married!"

"Let me explain. Just put the gun down… please," he tried to negotiate his way out.

"You're not in a position to give any requests."

I gripped the gun tighter and put my finger on the trigger. I was about to take his whole dome off.

"You better talk. You got sixty seconds," I said, aiming the pistol right at his head.

"Can you put the gun down?"

"Fifty-eight."

"Zykiah, I love you."

"Fifty-six. When were you going to inform me? Huh?" I asked, aiming the barrel to his head.

"Babe, I don't know."

"You better come up with something because time is running out.

Forty-five," I said, pointing at my watch.

"Okay. Yeah, I'm married to that crazy bitch. The reason I didn't tell you is because things were moving fast. I've been trying to get her to sign the papers."

I wanted to believe him, but he could've just came to

me and been straight up honest with me.

"Let me grab something out of my bag."

"Go ahead, but if you try something wild, I'm gonna bust you. So, think before you make a move," I said.

He grabbed his jacket, pulled a small envelope out, and took out some papers. I quickly scanned the papers. It was a court hearing scheduled for September 19th. He pointed to the box that indicated that the other party was not responding or cooperating. I was relieved to see those papers. I tossed the gun into the corner.

"Woo," Aubrey said, wiping the pound of sweat off his face.

"Come here," I commanded.

We kissed so passionately that our tongues were fighting in my mouth. I can't lie, I would've missed him a lot.

"It was about to be over with for your ass if you wouldn't have shown me them papers," I told him.

"Babe, I love you so much. Words can't describe how I feel about you," he said.

"No more secrets," I said.

"No more secrets. I promise," he replied.

I turned to him and motioned for him to come pound my pussy up. He kissed me passionately, and we fucked for over an hour. After we were done, we lay there until we fell asleep.

# Chapter 30

## Monica

Once I left Zykiah's house, I went straight to the Contour Day Spa. I got the full body treatment. I had a lot of tension built up within the last couple of hours. *It's always something,* I thought while the masseuse's powerful hands massaged my neck area. The cryotherapy facial and deep-tissue massage were out of this world. I kind of felt like I'd reached my breaking point.

"Mmm," I moaned. He was hitting every spot. I used to come here at least once a week.

The moon was sparkling in the sky when I left the spa. I grabbed my purse to check on Zykiah because she was on my mind. The first time I called, she didn't pick up.

"Shit, I hope things didn't go wrong."

I quickly built that stress back up. When I was about to dial her number again, I got an incoming call. It was her, so I swiped the accept icon immediately.

"Kiah, you good, boo?" I rushed into the conversation.

"Yeah, I'm good. I couldn't do it," she confessed, so I

knew she was deeply in love with him.

"What happened?" I asked.

Zykiah broke every detail down about what happened. She told me she was a second from blowing his head off. I felt her pain because men didn't realize how traumatic it could be for a woman dealing with so much. She assured me that once she got her hands on Kim, that would be the last time she'd breathe. We both had issues with that thot ass bitch.

"We going to make sure she'll never walk this earth again," I said.

"After I'm done with her, she won't be able to walk in heaven or hell."

"I know that's right," I agreed.

Kiah talked to me until I pulled into my driveway.

"Hold on, Zykiah. I pulled up at my place."

I held the phone on one side of my ear as I grabbed my purse and headed toward my front door.

As I was walking to the door, I felt kind of weird about something, but I couldn't put my finger on it. *Maybe it's just me,* I thought. Zykiah was beating my ear up about how much she was in love with Aubrey, and I was taking it all in. When I put the key in the door, I was struck in the back of my head and fell out cold.

Six Hours Later

When I woke up, I was chained to a metal chair. *What the hell happened?* My mind was spinning ridiculously. I didn't know where I was. My face felt like it'd been hit with a thousand bricks. I could feel the blood dripping from my mouth. I spit all the blood onto the ground. It was freezing cold. It felt like it was snowing in this bitch

"Well, well… What do we have here?"

I heard a voice coming from a far distance, but it was getting closer to me. Whoever was walking toward me had a metal object that was hitting the ground.

"You think you can just walk away?"

*BANG!*

The object hit the ground, causing me to jump. At this point, it sounded like a pipe or something similar. My nerves were boiling up because I didn't know what was going on.

"I just want out," I finally said to whoever it was.

I shifted my body in an attempt to find this mystery person.

"Why are you doing this to me?"

Tears were running from my eyes. I felt like I might not make it this time. My life flashed before my eyes. I saw the past then my future.

"It's just not that easy, Mrs. Carter."

I knew I had heard that voice before, but I couldn't picture who it belonged to.

"Who are y—" I was cut off with a blow to the face, then I was out again.

# Chapter 31

## Marcus

Sitting at the Sunset Grill, I waited on my partner, Amber, to arrive so we could have lunch and get back on the right path. We needed to connect all the pieces of these crazy homicides. The Sunset Grill was more packed than usual for a Tuesday afternoon. As I waited, I dialed Monica's number, but it went straight to voicemail. I tried one more time and got the same response. That was odd. She always kept her phone charged in case of emergency. When I was about to call Zykiah, Amber came walking in, so I just pushed it to the side. I'd try again later. Amber had her black detective shirt on with some khaki pants. I pulled her chair out, being a gentleman.

"Hi, Amber, how are you?" I asked.

"Fine. Just trying to soak everything in," she responded.

There was something about her. The vibe wasn't right.

"These past couple of days, we ain't be—"

She cut me off. "Yeah, I would like to apologize for that."

She grabbed my hand and patted me on the back.

"So, we good?"

"Of course," she replied.

I grabbed the menu and waited for someone to come and take our order.

"How may I help you?" the waiter asked as he took his pen and paper out.

I could see his name tag said "Elijah."

"I will have a grilled burger today."

"If I were you, I'd get the house," Elijah suggested.

He explained that the house had the same grill burger but with potato tots for one dollar more.

"I'll take the house, then."

I ordered it with lemonade. I wanted something stronger, but I needed to replenish my body. He then turned to Amber.

"I will have a fish salad," she said.

He took our menus and went to the back. I just stared at her for a quick second. There was something about her, but I couldn't put my finger on it. It didn't take long for Elijah to bring our meals to the table. The house was worth the money. The plate was loaded with potato tots with chopped onions. The fish salad Amber had looked okay, but there could have been more.

"That's what you wanted?" I pointed at the weird ass looking salad.

"Of course. You know I'm working on my figure," she said and stood up.

I just shook my head because she wasn't that big. If she lost any more weight, she would disappear. I laughed to myself.

"I'm still shocked about Chief Bryant!" I expressed.

"Me too. It's getting horrible out there. How are you and ole girl doing?" she asked, snapping her fingers, trying to remember her name.

"Monica. We good," I shot back, wondering why her name came up.

"That's good y'all are doing good. Just make sure she ain't playing with you. Remember what happened with Yakika."

"Naw, Monica's different. We talk about everything," I defended her honor.

"I guess. Just be careful because people have secrets," she said and gave me a wink.

I sat there thinking, *would she keep something from me? No, she wouldn't.* I started battling with my thoughts.

"So, what's the update on Chief's case?" I asked.

"From what I know, there are no fingerprints," she

responded.

We sat there discussing the different cases for a good hour. Her demeanor changed every time I mentioned Chief Bryant. I wondered why. I gave her the details of my weekend in Miami. She told me she always wanted to meet Plies. I was shocked that this plain Jane white woman would know something about Plies. She also said she was a huge fan of Trina

Her phone rang, and she picked up but didn't say much. Once she hung up, she stood to her feet.

"I gotta go!" she didn't wait for my response.

She threw some money on the table and got the hell up out of there.

"Well, damn!" I said.

I noticed a small piece of paper on the floor. I picked it up and read it. It had an address on it. I tried to call Amber to give it to her, but she was gone, so I just tucked it away in my pocket. I sat there thinking about the meeting we just had. It was good that we were speaking again, but then again, Amber had something up with her. I motioned for Elijah to bring me a shot of Cîroc. While he was getting it, I tried to call Monica, and it was still going to voicemail. *This is not like her,* I thought myself. I sat there, pondering about things while drinking my cup of Cîroc. When I was about to take my last swallow, my phone rang. I got excited and thought it was my baby.

"Hello!" I said, sounding overly excited.

"Marcus, this Kiah. Mo with you?"

"No, I've been calling her phone all morning," I informed her.

"Same here. I'm pulling into her driveway now."

At this point, I was getting nervous because if Kiah didn't know what was going on, then something was wrong.

"All of her cars are here," she told me.

My alerts started to go off in my head. *I hope nothing's wrong with my baby,* I thought.

"Marcus!"

"Zykiah! Zykiah, what's wrong?"

The anticipation was driving me insane. My head started pounding.

"Marcus, her phone is broke into pieces, and her purse is still here."

I could hear the hurt in her voice. The tears fell from my eyes. I jumped up, ran to my car and sped off on a mission to find my baby.

# Chapter 32

## Monica

"What have I gotten myself into?" I asked myself. My body was in so much pain. I wondered if I would ever see my family again. That's all I kept playing in my head. I started praying because if this was going to be it, I needed to ask God for forgiveness. Right when I was about to say his name, the devil was walking in the door. I knew it was the devil because every time he or she came to check on me, I heard that same pipe hitting the ground. I didn't say anything. I could feel a body standing right over me. I was scared out of my fucking mind. I was weak. I hadn't had anything to eat. I'd been in here for God knows how long.

"It's crazy how people just think you're an angel," the devil said while revealing my head from under the pillowcase. The light blurred my vision. I couldn't rub them due to my hands being chained up.

"We can work something out," I pleaded for my life.

"Maybe. If you kill him."

"Him who?" I questioned.

"Marcus!" the devil said and pulled the face mask off

her face.

I was shocked that the person standing before me was Detective McDonald, holding a large metal pipe in her hand. It was her the whole time. The events started playing out in my head. She was how I was able to get in the people's houses. I felt like such a stupid ass bitch. Just when I was about to say something... *WHAM! WHAM!*

A powerful right punch hit my face then a slight left. I had blood flying from my mouth. I couldn't do anything about it. I just prayed that I didn't die there. She continued to slap me around like a rag doll. I saw nothing but stars when my eyes were closed. It was impossible for me to see. Suddenly, the cold barrel pressed against my head. Instantly, I saw all the faces I put in the same position. The only voice I heard was my grandmother's.

"It's not your time yet." The sound of my grandma's voice echoed in my ears.

The voice gave me the strength to endure the punishment that was forced upon me. Suddenly, the cold barrel wasn't on me anymore. I couldn't see, but I heard her leave the room. I tugged on the chains, trying to squeeze out of them. She had them on super tight. I didn't have any energy. I just sat there, waiting to see my maker. Then, I heard voices. My heart started pounding because I knew it was over until the voice got closer.

"Monica! Monica, no… no!" I knew that voice.

I heard footsteps getting to me.

"Baby, it's gonna be ok!."

I was totally out of it until I felt his hands touching my face.

"Mmm," I whined.

I didn't have the energy to say anything.

"It's me, baby!" Marcus said, trying to free my hands. Somehow, he couldn't.

"I got y—" He was cut off.

I heard his body hit the ground. Everything was blurry, so I couldn't see what was going on.

"You asked for this, Marcus!" she said.

"Amber, what are you doing?" Marcus asked.

"Since you want this bitch, you're gonna die with this bitch!"

"Kill me. Let her go," he pleaded.

His words filled my heart up. Somehow, my vision was clear enough to see what was going on. She had him on his knees begging for his life.

"You love her that much, huh?"

"C'mon, Amber. Why you doing this?" he asked, holding his hands up.

"First off, me and this bitch had a deal. She refused to continue," she said aggressively.

I was praying that she didn't kill him. Marcus had a confused look on his face because he didn't understand what kind of business Amber and I had going on.

"Well, you're blind to the fact that the little angel you claim to love has been keeping shit from you."

"What are you saying?"

"The murders in the city are the work of her hands."

His face dropped to the ground because he could not digest what he just heard.

"Yup, I hired the bitch to kill the motherfuckers that were responsible for my husband's death, including that meathead, Chief Bryant."

She was caught up in her emotions, and that's when Marcus rushed at her.

*POW!*

A shot went off, and the bullet hit him in the shoulder. He was landing combos left and right to her ass, but the white bitch did some kind of ninja move that laid him out. She grabbed the gun and stood over him. I thought he was dead. I could see the evil in her eyes.

"This is how you're going to end it, huh?" he asked.

She had the gun aimed at his head. He applied

pressure to his wounded shoulder.

"Take one last look at that bitch because it's over with for you and her," she said, gripping the trigger tight.

*POW! POW!*

It felt like everything happened in slow motion. My heart and mind were running everywhere. When I opened my eyes, Zykiah had a gun. She stood over Amber like a superhero. She shot her two more times to seal the deal.

"I'm here, Mo," she said and shot the chains off me.

The chains hit the floor. She wrapped her arms around me. Zykiah was my life saver. We hugged each other.

"Mo, I'm sorry this happened to you." We hugged one last time before we went to help Marcus. He was woozy, and blood was pouring out of his shoulder, but that didn't stop him. He still kissed me passionately. I pulled away, and I stared at him.

"Marcus, I'm sorry for—"

He cut me off. "Let it go, baby. Let's go home."

Zykiah helped us both get out. The bright light shined in my eyes and made it impossible to see. Zykiah gave me some shades out of her pocket. We proceeded to the car. Marcus and I sat in the back seat as Kiah took control of the car.

# Chapter 33

## Monica

### One Week Later

Kim and I sat at the crib watching reruns of *Martin.* I didn't care how much you watched *Martin*, you could still laugh like it was the first time you'd ever seen it. I'd been sitting at home for the past week since my kidnapping, taking things in. Kim was telling me how she was planning on moving out of Albany to Texas where the rest of her family lived. I just listened to her go on and on about things that were irrelevant to me.

"Kim, would you do me a favor?" I asked.

"Anything for you, friend," she said and patted my thigh.

"Go in the closet in my room and grab that black bag for me."

"Which one?"

"The second room."

Kim got up and went into the other room. I crept behind, making no noise. I texted Zykiah and told her to come on. My plan was in full effect. She held a picture of Jihad. I knew she was emotional. Her face was priceless.

I wish I had a camera to capture the moment.

"Monica," Kim said emotionally.

"Bitch, don't play like you're innocent."

She was standing there with a dumb ass look on her face. I wanted to just end her life right there, but that would take all thc fun out of things.

"You think I didn't know about you and Jihad? Bitch, I've been plotting on killing you ever since I first met you at the DMV."

Her eyes got wide as things started to come back to her.

"Monica, I'm sorry."

"Don't *sorry* me now, trifling ass hoe."

Out of nowhere, Zykiah bum-rushed her into the wall and hit her with a two-piece to her face.

"Bitch, you tried to kill me!" Zykiah yelled while kicking her in the stomach.

Kim was leaking from her mouth. Just when we thought she was out, Kim snapped back and charged at Zykiah, pinning her against the wall and giving her a light blow. I knew my girl was going to snap back, but I came from the back and clocked the bitch in the head with the butt of my gun. Zykiah kicked her dead in the face. Kim was out cold. She snatched the gun out of my hand and pressed it against her head. Things were getting hectic. Kim was not stable. Her blood was all over the floor.

"Zykiah!" I screamed.

She turned toward me.

"Zykiah, stop."

"Mo! It's not that simple," she said.

"She ain't even worth it."

I grabbed the hand she had the gun in and stared her in her eyes. I saw the pain in them. As much as I wanted to send her world crashing down, it wasn't worth it.

"Mo, it's deeper than that. I can't let it go."

"Why?" I asked.

"She won't sign the papers."

I grabbed a handful of her hair and told her that she was going to sign the divorce papers, and if she didn't, her life was going to be over. Kiah gave me the gun and told me to hold on to it while she got the forms and a pen. I kept the gun aimed at Kim until Kiah came back. When Kiah came back, she handed Kim the form that needed to be signed.

"Bitch, sign or die," she demanded of her.

Kim did what she was told. I could see the relief on her face after Kim had signed. Kiah punched Kim one last time, knocking her out. I dragged her ass to my car and dumped her back at her house in the bushes.  As we drove back to my place, Kiah called Aubrey up and told him the good news. I could see the love and happiness in Kiah's eyes.

# Epilogue

## Monica

### Six Years Later

I had just arrived in Albany and was headed to the cemetery to visit Chief Bryant's grave with Marcus. We'd been coming back every year to pay tribute to him. Marcus and I stepped out of the BMW X6 and walked to the grave site. Marcus was shedding tears like always. I just wiped his tears away.

"Well, Chief, it's me again. I came to let you know I miss you like crazy. I was never a big talker, but this might be the last time I come visit you. You will always be in my heart," Marcus said with tears running down his face.

I just stood back and let him have his moment.

"Mama, why Daddy crying?" Dakota asked.

"Daddy just had to let his past go."

I kissed her on the forehead. She was still lost and had no clue what I meant. Marcus came to the car where we were waiting, got in, and we left it all behind.

After all the pain and betrayal that I had suffered, I was happily married with a five-year-old daughter. Kiah and I had been married for six years, and after marrying the men of our dreams, we all decided the best thing to do was move away from Albany. Marcus and Aubrey started a sports bar together while Kiah and I opened a restaurant called Diva's Palace which was located in Savannah. I was the happiest woman on Earth. I was married to a wonderful man, and I had a beautiful daughter. After all the heartbreak and pain I had endured, I knew I wouldn't have to go through that type of pain ever again. As I stared into my husband's eyes, I could see the love there. As our lips met, I knew that falling in love with Marcus was the best choice that I had ever made.

*The End*

## Acknowledgments

First, I give all my praise to the highest God for blessing me in so many ways. To my mother, Bessie Thornton, the most beautiful woman God could have ever created. Thank you for always telling me to read. Thank you for your support during this entire journey.

To my grandma, Mrs. Jewell Walker, I miss you so much. I know you are watching me from the sky.

Also, I'd like to give thanks to a guy I've known all my life, Aubrey "Blackboi" Rolle, for encouraging me the whole way through this book. Thank you, homie. If it weren't for you, I probably wouldn't have ever finished. I love you like a brother. To Ms. Ebony Bryant, thank you for everything; you have been a blessing in my life. Thank you :-) To my brothers, Mike and Chris, yo' lil bro luv you! Everything is going to be okay. I promise I got us! To my lil' cousins, Yasmen, Tye, EJ, JT, Big Man, Dee, Big Ma, Boo, Freddy, and the rest of Pam's kids, I love y'all so much. I want y'all to be great! Zykiah, thank you for being a good friend. To my Favorite LIL' BIG CUZ, Lovetta Brown, I miss you. I'm proud of you too. To all my nieces and nephews, I love you y'all. To Neil Lewis, Yokubi (N.O), Shawty Lo, Hellboi, Ant Smith (best roommate ever, appreciate everything), Marquette, Jabo, Snoop, 229 crew, Quiet, Slim, and everyone that gave me any type of inspiration, thank you! Eric T, Money, Vess Tyson, Tra William, Harry Jackson, Big G, Dirty D, the whole F2, thank you! Sapp, I appreciate you, bruh, for helping me with my law work. You came through for da kid!

To MAJOR KEY PUBLISHING, thank you for giving me a chance to broadcast my talent.

The SKY IS THE LIMIT

# CONNECT WITH ME ON SOCIAL MEDIA

**Facebook Personal Page:** Author King Nikalos

**Facebook Author Page:** Author King Nikalos

**Instagram:** KingNikalos

## About the Author

Nikalos was born in Albany, Georgia. His mother is his greatest inspiration and always encourages him to be the best writer that he can be. He fell in love with reading and writing romance at an early age, but never dreamed that he was going to be an author. Right now, Nikalos is the author of Trapped Between the Two: A lustful Love Triangle and is currently working on his next book. His dream is to be the best writer that he can be and entertain each and every one of his readers.

Be sure to LIKE our Major Key Publishing

page on Facebook!

CPSIA information can be obtained
at www.ICGtesting.com
Printed in the USA
LVOW10s2343190118
563260LV00021B/921/P